Other Books by Barbara Robidoux

Waiting for Rain (2007)
Migrant Moon (2012)

SWEETGRASS BURNING: STORIES FROM THE REZ

Santa Fe, NM

Dear Uncle –
Thank you for
your support over
the years –

love, Barbie

Copyright (c) 2016 by Robidoux, Barbara (1944 –)

Published in Massachusetts by Blue Hand Books, a publishing collective of Native American writers.

Blue Hand Books, 442 Main St. #1061, Greenfield, MA 01031

Formatting and Pre-Press: Pressbooks, Montreal, Canada

First Edition.

ISBN: 978-0692642351 (Blue Hand Books)(Paperback)

Cover Design: Barb Burke; Editor: Trace Hentz; Cover Photo: Barbara Robidoux

This book is dedicated to the people of the Rez. Every Rez.

And to Linda Hogan who supported the writing of these stories.

Contents

I

THE EDGE

Today I walk the half mile to the Super Saver, the only grocery store on the reservation. Sea smoke rises out of Passamaquoddy Bay, the frigid north Atlantic water warmer than the air. Fog shrouds houses along the shore. Snow thigh deep makes snowshoes the only sensible means of transportation. Drifts five and six feet high cover cars and anything else in their paths.

I stop along the way to check on old Gregory

who lives alone and is mostly blind. The door to his two room wooden house is painted bright yellow. "So I can always find it," he tells anyone who asks.

I take off my snowshoes and walk in without knocking. Greg is burning sweetgrass and the sweet smell of the smoke reminds me this is my home place. I make sure the wood stove is filled and ask if he needs any supplies.

"Just Lipton tea bags and a dozen eggs," he tells me. "Don't worry, Dous," he tells me sensing my anxiety about the weather. "Walk along the wooden fence. You can hold on if the wind tries to blow you over." Greg chuckles. I put on my snowshoes at the door, walk out his kitchen door and step into the blizzard.

I do as he says, breaking a trail with snowshoes in the deep snow along the fence line. We've both survived many a "Nor'easter" as they call these ferocious coastal storms. Gregory was a fisherman in his younger days. He fished from a canoe in the rough and unpredictable waters of the bay. Like magic, he knew where to find the fish. He said the noise of an outboard motor scared the fish away so he used his silent canoe.

Last summer we gathered sweetgrass together. We had a deal. He liked the baskets I made from sweetgrass and brown ash so he took me to the grass in exchange for baskets which he would give as gifts to the ladies he was "courting" on the rez. He'd guide me down Route 1 to Highway 89, at Lubec and we'd head out toward Campobello Island and Canada. The saltwater meets the fresh along tidal rivers here and the grass grows very tall. Even though Greg is blind, he senses where the grasses grow in the same way that he could find pollack in the bay.

When I reach the wide door of the Super Saver, I stoop once again to unbuckle my snowshoes. We thought the tribally run store would keep prices reasonable, but without competition, even the Indian owner gets top dollar for everything sold.

I put my wooden snowshoes in a shopping cart and search the aisles for molasses, flour, yellow-eyed beans, cans of hominy, and Greg's tea bags and eggs. I plan to make hulled corn soup for supper with molasses cake for dessert. There will be enough to share with Greg. He loves the corn and bean soup, a tradition here, and molasses cake is his favorite way to satisfy his sweet tooth.

After stopping back to deliver Greg's food, I find he is taking his afternoon nap so I cross over the empty lot to the elderly housing to visit with Peg. She is sick with cancer. If she's feeling well enough, we'll play a couple of hands of cribbage. When she is feeling OK she can still beat me. She used to be known as "Cribbage Queen" of the rez, but today we don't play. Peg is not feeling well so we just visit for a while.

Elderly housing is located in a large brick apartment building between the elementary school and St. Anne's Catholic Church. The elder's apartments in the back of the building have large windows which face the shore. The elderly meal site is also located here. There is a large kitchen and cafeteria where meals are served at lunchtime five days a week. But no meals have been served here all week. Tonight is the last night of the four-day wake which is being held for the tribal governor who was killed suddenly when his pickup skidded on black ice. He was on his way home from Indian Island and a council meeting with the Penobscots. His truck went off the road and plowed into some huge pine trees and he was killed.

George was laid out at the elderly meal site because it is the only place on the reservation large enough to hold the huge crowd of mourners who came to say goodbye. Usually people are waked in their homes but, he was a very popular guy all around the state of Maine. Even the governor of the state is expected to attend his funeral. That is, if he can make it to the rez in this blizzard. With George laid out at the meal site I walk down the hall to apartment #4, Peg's home, and since I hear music inside, I open the door and yell, "Hello."

Peg is laying on her couch listening to country music on KSIP, the tribal radio station. They take calls for requests and she is a regular call-in listener.

"Hi Tus, how you feeling?" I ask. "Like a piece of shit," is the reply. "It's the damn chemotherapy," Peg mumbles. "I'd rather die than take more of that poison into my body."

I don't respond right away. I don't want to think about Peg dying. Not now. She has been like a mother to me since my own mother's death. They were good friends and when mom was killed in a car wreck one icy winter night; I was sixteen and devastated.

Peg stood up and took care of me. It was eight years ago. My mom and I had a rocky relationship. Her drinking created a wall in between us. I never knew my father, he left before I was even born and all mom ever said about him was that he "couldn't take reservation life." Peg watched over me and was damned determined that I would not follow in my mother's alcoholic footsteps.

In her day, Peg was a looker and she liked to party, too, but she knew when to stop. Now her jet-black hair had turned completely white. It seemed to happen overnight with the diagnosis of stage four colon cancer and it sunk right in to her that she would die. When the cancer doctor told her she only had months to live, she looked him in the eye and yelled, "You go to hell!"

But her body turned against her will to live. She hardly ate and only slept with the help of sleeping pills. "My new bedfellows," she joked, holding up the bottle so I could see the morphine prescription on the label.

"Can I make you some tea, Tus?" I ask.

"That would be nice."

I set a pot of water to boil in her tiny kitchen. I ask, "How about some of the herbs Thompson sent over from Township?"

"Yes, that's good." Peg knew the herbs had helped others with cancer and as bitter as they tasted, she drank them several times a day. Thompson lives at Indian Township and provides the tribe with his knowledge of healing herbs. He is an old medicine man who drinks too much alcohol but he knows the plants. He knows where they grow and how to gather them and he prepares them in the old way with the prayers and songs that invite the herbs to heal. Peg and Thompson were lovers for years even though she is 20 years his younger. But after she got sick, he stopped coming around, just sent the herbs. Johnson is a womanizer and Peg's sickness did not set well with him. I sit in the rocker near Peg while the medicine tea cooks. The pungent odor of the herbs drifts towards us.

"Remember October year before last when you shot a moose at Alder Stream and we had to butcher it in a hurry?" I ask Peg, now unable to even lift a rifle.

"What a bloody mess!" she replies.

We had no electricity at Alder Stream camp, so we had to pack the meat with cedar boughs in a birch bark wigwam to keep it cool while we butchered.

"That moose fed a lot of people last year," she said.

"I remember when I got the phone call. You said, 'Dous, get over here and bring your knives. But first, see if you can find a chest freezer where we can store a moose.'"

It was at least a four-hour drive from where I was living to Alder Stream camp, but I made it there in three hours, I was so excited. It was an unusually warm October. I knew we had to get that moose butchered, packaged and frozen without delay.

I had to stop at the General Store in Searsmont for gas and while there I picked up an Uncle Henry's Swap or Sell It Guide. I checked for used appliances and I found this ad:

Chest freezer, large, works perfect,
white, clean, no frost.
$100 OBO leave message 315-6300.

Then I went outside to the pay phone and called my neighbor. No way could I fit a chest freezer and a cut up moose in the back of my Chevy Luv pickup.

"Check this out, will you?" I said to him. "If it's decent, buy it. I'll be home in two days or less. We're going to have moose meat this winter!"

We cut moose meat for 16 hours straight. We worked in four-hour shifts. A guy who lived down the road helped out in exchange for meat. He owned sharp knives and had a way with them for butchering. He'd been a butcher for years in Bangor and then decided to give it up and move to the deep woods. He jumped at the chance for fresh moose meat. However, after all that blood from butchering, for about a week, all I could eat was peanut butter and jelly sandwiches. Still, that moose fed several families that winter.

The odor of the tea drifts into the living room and I get up to check the roots simmering in the pan. The kitchen smells of the bitter herbs that have completely given themselves to the boiling water. I strain the tea and bring a cup to Peg, who by now has turned off the radio and is ready for our chat.

Peg used to be a stocky woman. Not fat but solid. Her ruddy brown face would beam in laughter or at times in anger. She could shoot a moose, quarter it in the woods, and haul it out on her back in brown ash pack baskets if there was no four-wheeler available to help. In spring she picked fiddle head ferns in the wetlands with black flies biting fierce as hornets even as the damp spring cold penetrated her bones. She'd sell them roadside or give them to family and friends. Fiddleheads are a favorite spring tonic that are known to rejuvenate the blood after a long winter without greens. At Christmas she made wreaths of balsam fir boughs and sold them to family and friends.

As I said, Peg was once stocky but now she is barely skin and bones. The cancer has robbed her vitality. Unable to eat, she has withered to a fraction of her self.

"Look at my legs, Dous," she said a few weeks

ago, "I never thought I'd end up with chicken legs."

Peg sleeps on the couch. Two windows look west to the bay. White caps roll onto the icy shore. The snow has let up and the low light of evening is beginning to darken.

I go back into the kitchen. There is a small wooden table covered with a flowered oilcloth and two chairs facing a window overlooking the Passamaquoddy Bay. Peg rarely sits here now. I turn off the flames under the pot of herbs and cover it. Peg sleeps on the old blue couch covered by a colorful knitted afghan she made last winter. I'll let her rest.

I leave Peg to her dreams and step outside. The snow has let up and the low light of evening is beginning to give way to darkness. A deep cold hits my face like a hard stinging slap. Often the coldest weather sets in after these northeastern winter storms. I head straight up the hill to the two-room cabin where I live. It's past time to feed the wood stove, my only source of heat.

When I approach my cabin, I pass the outhouse. It is there that I feel someone is watching me. It is an uncomfortable feeling. I look back to see who followed but there is no one there. Then I see him on the roof of the outhouse. A snowy owl. I meet the eyes of the great pure white owl. Its eyes are yellow, its beak black and its feet heavily feathered. Our eyes meet and I shiver. The owl sits and watches. It does not move. I had heard that a snowy owl had been seen by children playing at the shore last week. Some of the elders felt that the owl was sick and could not hunt for itself. Worried, they had put fish out on the snow to feed it. Had the great white owl come to die among us? Shaken, I continue along the path to my cabin and the warmth of my fire.

The cabin is small but cozy, just a living room, kitchen, and loft bed. The cast iron wood stove sits along the north wall in the living room and provides the best heat for chilled bones. It also gives me great emotional comfort. There is electricity but no plumbing, so I haul water from wherever I can. I thought of having a well dug but the thought is as far as it went. The tribal water supply tastes bad and some say it is polluted. When I want a hot bath I go over to my friends' homes. Most of the time "cat baths" are just fine with me. The view from my living room window is worth all the plumbing in the world. I can see First Island and Canada on a clear day. Finback whales migrate through here in summer and porpoise live in the bay. But the waters are not full of life like the old days Greg talks about— when there were so many fish that you could fish with your hands. Pollack were plentiful. Still, fish and clams remain. And all around them the wild blueberries, strawberries, and blackberries grow in the fields. I am so thankful for the gifts here. I feed the wood stove a mix of dry ash, pine and fir to get it going again.

A sweetgrass braid rests on the mantel behind the stove. Greg and I gathered it last summer. I light the end of the braid and the sweet aroma of the grass, unlike any other, fills the room. Smoke rises with my prayers for Peg, for Greg and for all those who are suffering. I am tired now and I rest in the rocker next to the stove.

Tomorrow, we will bury George. In the old days if someone died in winter, the men would build a bonfire to melt the snow and thaw the earth before they could dig the grave with shovels. His grave will be dug with a backhoe. And his sons and nephews will carry his body from the Mass at St. Anne's up the hill past the elderly to the cemetery. Prayer songs will be sung and he will be put to rest. Most tribal members will be there to say their goodbyes.

The next morning, we never see the sun rise. The storm lingers. Now there are several feet of snow covering our world. The wind has formed drifts four and five feet high during the night. The coffin is carried from the church on two wide toboggans tied together. Several men spend time at the cemetery digging the snow out of his grave while Father Sullivan says Mass at St. Anne's. George's family includes a great number of tribal members and friends who trudge through the snow up the hill from the church to the cemetery. The six pallbearers take turns pulling the toboggans that carry his body to his grave. The state dignitaries we expected are unable to make it through the storm to his funeral. Even the *Bangor Daily News* and *Quoddy Tides* newspaper reporters are snowed out.

I sleep late and missed the Mass but make it to the cemetery in time to watch George's coffin being lowered slowly into his grave. Someone has brought some red roses. We take turns throwing them in the grave before the backhoe covers it with frozen earth and snow. On the way home I check on Peg. With the power off in the night, I'm afraid her heater isn't working. When I enter the front door of the apartment complex, I realize it is as cold inside as it is outside. I walk down the hall and listen at her door. No sounds come from the other side.

"Peg, you alright?"

No answer.

I knock on the door this time calling louder, "Peg, you in there?" But still there is no answer. My heart beats faster and faster. I turn the doorknob and walk in.

Peg isn't on the couch, her usual resting place, and the room is cold enough for me to see my frozen breath. I check the kitchen, the tiny bathroom, and the bedroom which she rarely uses now.

Peg is missing. But I don't know how she could have left in this storm? I sit down on the couch. Her pillows and blankets are in disarray.

Then I notice a scrap of paper next to the radio on her small table.

SEE YOU LATER. LOVE, P

My heart begins to race again. The phone lines don't work due to the storm, so I can't call Tribal Police. But I desperately need to find her or get in touch with someone. All I can do is go over to Gregory's. I go out and plow through the deep snow while my mind races with questions. Where is she? How could she have left in this storm?

Storm clouds lay heavy on the water when I burst into Greg's house. He is an early riser, and he sits at his round wooden table next to his kitchen stove drinking a cup of tea. His favorite blue enamel teacup warm his wrinkled brown hand. He is looking out the window that faces the bay. Greg isn't startled. In fact he acts as if he knew I was coming.

"It's Peg," I blurt out. "She's gone." Peg is my lifeline. Without her, even in her weakened state, I feared I'd lose my compass, my map. Who would be there to guide me when I strayed off course?

"I know, saw her in the early light walking all

alone by the shore. She was at the edge where the tide had washed the snow away. She's alright now."

Tears streaming down my face, I know Greg is right.

2

FISHING THE OLD SOW

When spring finally did arrive, the land softened and became saturated with water. What had been frozen white gave itself over to green. Spruce buds opened and the old trees became young again. At Francis Point the birch trees leafed out and drank in the salty air after a long thirsty winter. Along the shore, the sandy beach appeared after months hidden under thick ice. Hungry black bears came out of their long sleep and roamed the reservation. One day I was at the health center waiting to see a nurse and a friend came looking for me.

"Dous," he said, "you've got company at your house."

"Who?" I asked.

"I just saw three back bears walking out of your driveway"

"Well, I better get home then."

At Mirror Lake the ice thawed and we all made guesses about when it would actually happen; when the bottom of the lake would rise to the top and the top would go under. We took bets on "ice out" days.

This year old Greg won when he guessed April 15th. The prize was a twenty-five-dollar certificate for food at the Super Saver. He was overjoyed and bought steaks and potatoes with the money. Then I cooked us dinner and baked a blueberry pie for dessert with wild blueberries I had canned last summer.

First and Second Islands began to green and we all watched their transformation. Sea birds returned and the land birds followed. We yearned to take picnics of sardines and saltine crackers and cheese and baloney sandwiches with our kids in tow to the light house at Quoddy Head. After the long winter, our blood flowed freely.

Then the spring fog began to settle into our bones. We needed to navigate our lives with caution. With spring the sea creatures returned. Some called them monsters or dragons; others saw them as messengers from another world. Old women went down to the shore and watched. In the distance of the bay they showed themselves to each other. When a water creature was spotted, the women sang a welcoming song.

The spring after Peg died brought heavy rains and floods. Early one morning, driving Rte 190 off the rez, I had to open the driver's door and watch the yellow dividing line to stay on the road. Luckily Greg was with me when I nearly drove off the causeway bridge. If he hadn't sensed danger and grabbed the wheel we both would have been fish food in the bay.

Eastport or "Beastport," as the town is unaffectionately called by some, is a small fishing village of whites that borders the reservation.

Like many towns adjacent to Indian land, its inhabitants hold themselves above their Indian neighbors except when it comes to sex. Unfortunately, some Indians have children with the beasts of Eastport. A few marry, but mostly the mixed-blood kids stay with their Indian mothers and are raised on the rez.

Ricky, the son of my friend Bonnie, is one of these kids with a foot in two worlds. He is an eighteen-year-old party animal who thinks he is hot shit. Last night Ricky had left home and walked or hitch hiked the six miles to Eastport where he had so-called friends. Greg and I were assigned the task of finding Ricky and hauling his ass home. His mother is too sick to do the job.

His mom, Bonnie, and I went to "Beastport High" together. We had no choice since the rez school only went to eighth grade. We became lifelong friends. When Bonnie got pregnant in our junior year by a white "beastie," I was there for her. She never told the guy when she started to show. She just dropped out of school and stayed away. No one thought much about it since the dropout rate was close to seventy percent at that school. Both Indians and whites figured school was a waste of their time and preferred to find work and make some money. Problem was, and still is, there is very little work around here. With unemployment near eighty percent on the rez, GA, or general assistance, is all we can hope for. That is unless we are lucky enough to have a relative elected to tribal government who will offer us a job.

I became Bonnie's birthing partner, and we attended birthing classes together at the IHS health center. I watched Ricky enter this world. He was born with a caul. He had the gift of seeing. Maybe that's why he is such a wild teenager who drinks too much alcohol and smokes too much weed. But he does know how to fish, and Greg and I figured we'd find him at the pier.

When Ricky was born, his birth sac covered his head. He was born with a veil and the old women said he would be different. He would be able to see things before they actually happened. They also said he would be an outstanding fisherman since he would be able to see where the fish were, and he would also be able to hear storms brewing before they hit. But most important, he would never have to fear death by drowning.

Bonnie had taken a turn for the worse lately. Her speech is slurred and her balance is off. She's been to four neurologists down in Bangor, but no one knows what is wrong. "They even sent my blood to Germany," she told me last week. "But nobody knows what is wrong with me. He wanted to send it to Japan but I said 'NO WAY!'" Last summer a medicine man told her that she had fallen and hit her head, but she has no memory of this.

So Greg and I were on a mission, and we knew it would not be easy. Even if we did find Ricky, we would have to convince him to come home with us. We decided to check the pier first, so we headed down Water Street. Here in the Quoddy Loop, the tides are extremely high and extremely low. This is the Bay of Fundy, which has a very large mouth and an ever-narrowing passageway to the head of the bay. The enormous volume of incoming tidal water is forwarded upward causing vast tidal differences. Sometimes over fifty feet. When you tie your boat up at Eastport Pier you'd better have a long line. Twice a day the tides come in and go out.

At the pier I parked the truck and looked around for a familiar face. The sun was beginning to burn through the fog, and it was warm enough for me to leave my jacket in the truck. As I was trying to take off my jacket, Greg vibed the place.

"He's not here," Greg said after a few minutes.

"How do you know? We haven't even looked around."

"He's out on the water," Greg said matter-of-factly.

"In this fog?"

"Believe me, Dous, Ricky is out there fishing. Just drive over to Dog Island."

Greg spoke in a voice I knew better than to question, so I backed the truck off the pier and we headed back down Water Street towards Dog Island. We passed some of the old homes of whaling captains who had lived here at the turn of the century. Many were in need of paint and some were in need of much, much more.

At the corner of Water and Clark streets, we

drove down a dead end gravel road which led to Dog Island. About a quarter mile down the road I stopped the truck. We were parked on a flat cliff overlooking the bay.

"You suppose Ricky is out there?" I asked.

"He's going towards the Old Sow," Greg answered.

"Oh my God!" I yelled. "Not in HIS boat. Is he crazy?"

The Old Sow is a whirlpool—the second largest in the world. They say it's about 250 feet in diameter. Besides the Sow itself, there are numerous "piglets": small and medium sized whirlpools which surround it. The Sow got its name from the churning, pig-like noises it makes. Sometimes it shoots up waves ten to seventeen-feet high. At least ten people have met their death in the waters there. One fisherman who survived his ordeal said, "I didn't mind so much being caught in it, but I did resent having to row uphill to get out." The Old Sow is most active before high tide.

"What's the tide, Dous?" Greg asked.

"About half-high," I replied.

"And where's the moon?"

"Just new."

We were experiencing a so-called "spring tide." A tide that is full on the new or full moon. The worst of all circumstances for someone to be fishing near the Old Sow!

I always keep a pair of binoculars in the glove box of the truck. I reached for them. Greg was already outside leaning on the hood of the truck. He looked like he was saying his prayers. I lifted the binoculars to my eyes and pointed them in the direction of the Old Sow. Sure enough, there was Ricky rowing his boat towards the whirlpool.

"Is he crazy?" I muttered. "He knows better."

"Lots of pollack out there," Greg answered. "With this moon and tide, the Sow will throw out plenty of fish. Ricky will be able to fill his boat in no time." Greg spoke as though talking to himself. He was off into his own world. Probably right in the boat with Ricky. In his day, Greg used to fish with his hands.

I was about to pee my pants, so I took a time out and found a bush. When I got back, I found Greg gathering twigs and dry spruce boughs.

"We havin' a cookout?" I asked.

"Yup. We're buildin' a smudge so he'll be able to get his bearin's."

"OK then."

I gathered more boughs and added them to Greg's pile.

"Got a match?" he asked.

"No, but here's a lighter." I heaped some dry pine and spruce boughs on top of Greg's twigs.

"There's a downed birch over there," I pointed. "I'll go get some bark."

Greg and I got a fire burning in short time. At first it was just flames from the dry twigs and pine needles, but after the birch bark caught hold we placed limbs of a dead spruce and then some boughs on top of the fire. We wanted smoke and we got it.

Meantime, Ricky's wooden dory, a double ended rowboat common to these waters, tossed and heaved in the choppy waters below us. He was a stubborn but good-natured child who spent most of his time at the shore digging clams, gathering mussels and "wrinkles" as he called periwinkles. He loved to build a fire at the shore and cook the wrinkles in a tin can with sea water until the snail was forced out of its shell. Then he feasted.

The wooden boat struggled against the powerful currents of the whirlpool. This was the first time he had been caught in the treacherous waters of the Old Sow. By now, I was sure his small boat was taking on water as the waves beat over its shallow sides.

If he stopped rowing to bail, he'd be in more trouble. His arms must ache; his rowing skills were tested in ways he had never encountered. I thought of the old woman who had prophesied that he would never die from drowning, but it was little consolation now. I feared the sea would take him after all.

"We've got to lure him back. The smoke will help him keep on course so he doesn't get turned around," Greg told me.

I picked up the binoculars and saw Ricky struggling to row his dory towards us. All of a sudden the boat turned and headed towards Deer Island and the Canadian shore.

"Where the hell is he going?" I yelled.

"To the Canadian side where the price for fish is higher," Greg answered.

"Well, he's on his own then," I told Greg. Neither of us possessed a passport card needed to cross from Calais, Maine, into Canada. Driver's licenses or tribal identification cards weren't enough anymore.

"We ought to have our own passports, like the Onandagas," I told Greg. "Indians never knew white man's boundaries. Like deer and moose and the fish in the bay, we just followed our noses and went wherever we wanted."

"Well, no sense waiting around here. He'll either turn up or he won't. Let's go get some lunch," Greg says, clearly annoyed. We put out the fire and headed back into town.

"I don't want to eat here," I told Greg. "Let's go to the Wab."

"Okay."

We drove the causeway back from Eastport to the rez. By now the sun was shining and it was warm enough to roll down the truck windows. The salt air filled our lungs.

"I could eat a moose," I told Greg.

"Yup."

The Wab or Wabanaki Café is a tribally run general store and café. The menu varies with the availability of wild meat and fresh fish. When there is nothing fresh caught they serve Hull Corn Soup, a traditional hearty soup of white corn and great northern beans. My stomach began to growl with the mention of food. We drove the five miles to the western edge of the reservation and pulled into the parking lot of the Wab. A group of young skins were hanging around an '89 red Chevy pick up with Canadian plates. They were very interested in something in the bed of the truck. Greg and I were too hungry to investigate.

Inside the Wab, country music blarred and the smell of fried fish hit our noses. We walked between the shelves of Campbell soups, saltine crackers, macaroni, and canned tomatoes to the back of the store and sat at the lunch counter.

"What's on special today?" I asked Eddie Francis who stood behind the counter. He wore a white apron and had a large knife in his hand.

"Special is fish sandwich with fries and coleslaw," he said with a wide grin.

"Pollack?" I asked.

"Yup. Fresh from Canada. Did you see them in the back of that pickup on your way in?"

"No. But I noticed the Canadian plates."

"A skicin, Indian, from here hauled in a dory full of fish just this morning over on Deer Island. Now they are peddling it over here."

"What else are they peddlin'?" I asked.

"Don't know, Dous. Alls I'm interested in is fish. At least for now," Eddie answered.

It was common for cigarettes, marijuana and other drugs to be transported back and forth between the US and Canada by fishermen. With cigarettes close to ten dollars a pack in Canada and only about five dollars in the U.S., there is money to be made smuggling cigarettes. Fish often served as camouflage for the smuggler/fisherman who couldn't make a living by fishing alone.

"Where'd those guys get that fish anyhow?" I asked. "I have no idea, Dous. All I know is from the smell and the taste they are fresh out of the bay. Why don't you ask them?"

I knew better than to question those guys. If they were smugglers, they would not have appreciated the interrogation one bit. But I did wonder if they were Ricky's fish.

3

VOICES OF OUR ANCESTORS

Part 1

After his fishing escapade, Ricky stayed away all spring. Bonnie was worried sick about him but at least we knew he was still alive and we all knew there was no convincing him to come home until he was good and ready. But his boat was never found. According to the old women's prophesy about him being born with a caul, we knew he wouldn't have drowned. Besides, old Greg covered for Ricky and insisted that those were his fish that were sold to the Wabanaki Café, and I trusted Greg's intuition about this.

Ricky could have been anywhere in Canada, or passing as a white man in Bangor with skin light enough to disguise his true identity. He's a man now, twenty-one-years-old and any trouble would throw him in jail without question if the authorities there knew he was a Northpoint Indian.

Bonnie did not want to put out a missing person alert on him. She felt sure he would come home. But her health took a turn for the worse. Her speech was slurred and her balance off. She walked with a cane. "I sound like I'm drunk," she complained to me. "And I don't even drink." Her voice rose in anger.

Then one foggy morning in early May, while driving to a Doctor's appointment in Machias, she misjudged the distance between the edge of the highway and the gravel ditch along the side of the road. She went down the embankment and her old Chevy Nova settled against a giant spruce. The tree survived, but her car was totaled. Luckily, she hit on the passenger side. This accident ended Bonnie's driving days. Shortly after that accident, her eyesight began to fail.

The first of June rolled around and it was Bonnie's forty-fifth birthday. On that Saturday, I planned to take her down to Indian Island to the high stakes Bingo game the Penobscots run. Bonnie loves to play bingo and it was my birthday present to her. It is a three-hour drive in good weather so we decided to leave early morning, have breakfast on the road and get there in time for the early bird special. Around 6 am, I drove over to Hollywood, the trailer park where Bonnie lives. I pulled up to her singlewide trailer and parked the truck. The tribe bought these trailers fifteen years ago after the housing director was charged with embezzlement and HUD put a freeze on housing funds. They were desperate to find housing for tribal members, so twenty trailers were hauled in and set up in a low-lying area near the tribal offices. Somebody named the place Hollywood and it stuck.

An early morning iridescent glow from first light turned everything it touched golden. The sun was about to rise out of the bay. The earth stood still. Even the waters seemed to listen. No birds sang. It was that time between night and day when only the light moves. When daylight enters the sky. Then in the east the sun rose out of the horizon, out of the ocean, and out of darkness into morning.

I climbed the steps to the door of Bonnie's trailer. I expected to see her light on inside but the windows were dark. Sometimes she slept through the noise of her alarm clock. I might have to wake her. I tried knocking, then the door knob. Locked. Luckily she had given me a key. "Just in case I need a back-up," she had said. I used my key to open the door and entered the dark room. Until my eyes adjusted to the dark I could barely see, but I smelled coffee brewing.

"Bon, you awake?"

She didn't answer. I walked through the small kitchen down a narrow hallway to Bonnie's bedroom."

"Bon, you awake?"

"I'm up, open the door."

Bonnie sat up in bed leaning against her pillows, her long, dark hair pulled back into a loose braid. She held a cup of coffee in one hand and a cigarette in the other. I was relieved.

"Happy birthday, Tus. Are we going to celebrate or not?"

Bonnie seemed to be in-between sleep and waking. She spoke softly, "I had a dream Ricky came home, but I wasn't here. So he left again. I missed him."

"Well, it's your day. We can stick around if you want to. Whatever you want to do."

"I want to go down to the shore and listen to the water. There's coffee in the kitchen, help yourself."

Bonnie and I are members of a group of concerned tribal members, mostly women, opposed to the building of a liquid natural gas plant on our tribal land. The tribal council voted to lease fourteen acres of ceremonial land along the shore to an Oklahoma-based natural gas company. We came together to oppose this dangerous deal. The threat to our community as well as to the neighboring towns from Canada clear to Machias and beyond could be staggering. In the event of an accident we would all be blown to bits. If liquid natural gas ruptures out of a damaged ship, the gas will vaporize. When it comes in contact with water and mixes with the atmosphere, the resulting mixture is highly explosive. The mixture could be blown several miles from a damaged ship to nearby land before it detonates. Given the currents and extreme tides of the waters of Quoddy Bay, the chances for one of their ships to be grounded or to take a hit on a rocky ledge are very good. These ships would also be traveling the waters around the Old Sow, the dangerous whirlpool. We feel it is our responsibility to take care of our land to ensure that our descendants have what they need to survive in a good way. Liquid natural gas does not fit into our vision for our future.

We have enemies. There are those who want the LNG company to build their quarter-mile pier into the waters of Passamaquoddy Bay. They say it would bring jobs into our community. But at what cost? The highly flammable gas transported by huge ships and barges into these waters would threaten our well-being. Those who support this deal try to silence us. The twelve-story-high storage tanks they want to build would stand on our ceremonial grounds. This is a sacred site and it is against our values to desecrate it in this way. The company has offered, in a feeble gesture of acknowledgment, to allow us to decorate these tanks with our art.

Bonnie may be physically weakened, but she is a spiritual warrior. Her charismatic way of speaking, her ability to stand with the ancestors to remind us of who we are threatens some in the tribe. Because the ancestors speak through her, those who want to forget the old ways want her silenced. Two years ago when she ran for tribal governor, someone planted a pipe bomb in her car, the green Chevy Nova. She received anonymous death threats. The perpetrators were never identified, but some say it was a tribal policeman who was behind it. He has much to gain from the LNG deal.

Bonnie pulled back the bedcovers and reached for her cane. "Dous, do you think I'm sick because they put a whammy on me," she asks before turning to limp into the kitchen.

The hairs on my arms stood up. "What do you mean?"

"Well, the doctors can't figure out what is wrong. And now Ricky has disappeared. You know how they work on family members too when they want to get at someone."

"Well, Bon, could be. Maybe you need a curing. Why not get dressed and we can talk about this down by the shore."

"OK," she said as she walked down the hall towards the bathroom.

People didn't talk about it, but we all knew when someone was witched. A house would burn to the ground for no apparent reason. Someone would lose a child to a terrible accident. A few years ago a triple murder/suicide occurred: John Neptune killed his son, then his wife, then took his hunting rifle and somehow killed himself all within an hour's time. John had been a gentle man but something took over him. He was not himself. The newspapers called it murder, but we all knew better.

I decided to step outside and wait for Bonnie in the truck. I needed to clear my head. I told Bonnie I'd go out and warm up the truck. By then, the sun had risen out of the bay. Soon the whales would return on their summer migration to feed in these waters. But if their deal goes through, huge ships will disturb this ancient passageway. The whales will be in danger if forced to share the waters with massive iron ships. Even the sea creatures might disappear. All sea life will be affected. Fishing, as we have known it from the time of our ancestors, will be gone. The sacred bond between the people and these waters that has sustained us all throughout our history will be broken. The old women will not stand for this.

We drive the short distance from Hollywood to Francis Point at the northern tip of the reservation. Here we are surrounded on three sides by the waters of Passamaquoddy Bay. Bonnie is quiet as I pull the truck onto the rocky shore. She sits watching the water. It is near low tide and the wind is nearly calm.

"I'm gonna walk a while, okay?" I say, opening the truck door. I feel she needs some time alone and so do I. I need to digest our change in plans. We need breathing space.

The salt air is invigorating. Coarse dark sand and pebbles stretch for miles at the edge of the cold Atlantic waters. As I walk I remember stories the old people told of whales with hands and feet who had lived with us in the long ago time. But the whales missed the sea, so eventually they returned there to live. They promised to show themselves to us when we sang honoring songs and asked for their help. We could use their help about now. Who would know the old songs? Would someone have to dream them?

When I was out of sight of Bonnie and the truck and had been walking for fifteen or twenty minutes in the distance, I see a large round black object that I am not able to identify. Something washed ashore. I was curious to find out what it was. It is not uncommon to find parts of wrecked boats, fallen trees, and even gear from some of the fishing boats that frequent these waters. But as I got closer I realized that I had come upon an enormous whale that had beached itself.

The whale lay peacefully on the beach as if it had come ashore to nap. Squawking seagulls hovered over it as if trying to wake the whale. I approached slowly. Is it alive or dead? As I got closer to the whale I was overcome by the smell of death. I coughed to rid my body of its putrid smell.

Its enormous dark body is forty or more feet long. There are white patches on its belly exposed to air. Its hairy head is about a quarter of the length of its body. Long dark hairs cover its lower lip and upper jaw. Horny growths protrude from its chin. Two blow holes on the top of its head tell me that this is a right whale. So rich in blubber it would have floated had it died at sea. It must have come ashore to die.

Its eye is closed but the mouth is open wide exposing hundreds of pairs of black baleen plates. Right whales are skimmers; they feed with their mouths open filtering krill through their baleen. I am sure this whale has come home to die.

Even so, the smell is nauseating. I leave it and return to Bonnie and the truck. I tell Bonnie about the whale, the huge mass of it, its closed eye and gigantic gaping mouth full of baleen. She just listens for a while then she says, "I wonder which one it is." There are tears in her eyes as she speaks.

"What do you mean?" I ask her.

"Let's just go see Greg."

Bonnie, like Greg, has a direct connection to the ancestors. I tease them sometimes about it. It's like they both have 1-800 numbers to dial up whenever they need to talk.

We drive over to Greg's to tell him about the whale. We pass St. Anne's red brick church and the Elderly Center and head up the hill to Greg's house. The few large trees on our reservation are starting to green and leaf out. Greg is sitting at his small wooden table overlooking the bay when we arrive. He is drinking from his blue enamel teacup with a Lipton tea bag string hanging over the edge.

"Greg, there's a whale beached near Francis Point!" I yell pushing my way through his door.

"Yes," he says. "I heard it."

Greg and Bonnie talk in their language, the old Northpoint language that I do not understand. I sit and listen for a long while.

They seem to travel to another place and I am mesmerized by the lyrical sounds of the ancient Northpoint words.

Two days later, marine biologists descend upon the whale. A tribal game warden called them for help with the whale and they decide to perform a necropsy in order to determine the cause of the whale's death. It is against our traditional ways to perform autopsies on our dead, human or animal. But in spite of this, the whale is taken from us. We are overcome with grief, then anger, then grief again until Greg tells us we have to let go and pray the spirit of our ancestor whale will have an easy passage.

A week later Greg gets a call telling him that when they opened the whale they found the head of an obsidian harpoon lodged close to its huge heart. It's been over 100 years since whales were hunted with harpoons like the one they found. This was a very old whale.

As our elder spokesperson, Greg asks for the bones of the whale to be returned to us. They agree. We wait for several weeks until one day he gets a call from the marine biologists who are ready to return the whalebones to us. When the bones arrive, we bury them in the cemetery up the hill from St. Anne's church where all tribal members are put to rest. But not without an argument with the priest who insists that in a Catholic cemetery this is unacceptable. Greg, our elder, tells him, "These are our burial grounds, not yours. Your bones will never rest here."

4

PART TWO

———

Ricky, Bonnie's son, returned to the reservation for our annual Indian Day celebrations in August. He told Bonnie he had been living in Calais working in a lumberyard, but she didn't believe him because he was about twenty pounds thinner and he looked sick. Bonnie suspected that Ricky had been using drugs, maybe even trafficking. This time it was more than just smoking weed. By his gaunt looks, she felt he had gotten into the hard stuff: coke, crack, maybe even meth. To Bonnie's disappointment, he only stayed around for the weekend, but he said he planned to come home soon and try to get a job laying pipeline or working on the liquid natural gas pier.

We had meeting after meeting and tried to stop it but despite our efforts to prevent it, in early September LNG moved in. They began work on their quarter mile pier near where I had found the dead right whale. Had the ancient whale offered itself? A sacrifice to stop this? But there was no stopping their development and our lives will be changed forever. It took only a matter of weeks before the LNG pier intruded into the waters of Passamaquoddy Bay. Soon huge ships transporting liquid natural gas were docked there. Their giant storage tanks held the gas.

That was in August and a little over a month later, on September 25th, a storm blew up the northeast coast. It showed up with fifty-foot seas, gale force winds more than 90 mph, and driving rain. Hitting hard at Gloucester, Massachusetts, hurricane winds destroyed roads, houses, and the shoreline. It threw a thirty-foot chunk of granite seawall weighing twenty tons into the sea. The storm was called *Hurricane Grace*. She traveled over the waters of New Hampshire and into Maine waters. At Portland, Maine, rain fell at the rate of four inches per hour with winds between ninety-five and one hundred miles per hour. By the time *Hurricane Grace* reached our reservation, she was a monster of a storm.

We are only eighty acres and surrounded on three sides by water. No one had seen a storm of this magnitude in over seventy-five years. Grace combined with two other storms into what was called the "Super Storm." A Gloucester fishing vessel named the Andrea Gale went down in 100 foot walls of water while fishing along the outer banks near Newfoundland. Captain and all crew members were lost at sea.

The hurricane hit us hard. Houses along the shore lost their roofs, trailers were over turned in Hollywood and the LNG pier was smashed to smithereens. Bonnie and I holed up at Greg's house and watched as white capped waves in the bay crashed into the shore. The thunderous sound of water and wind made it impossible to carry on a conversation so we just sat together holding on tight. Greg's little house swayed and moved with the force of the wind but in the end it held its ground.

Bonnie's trailer was another story. Her roof along with the roofs of several other homes at Hollywood blew away into the sea. My cabin stayed intact although my stovepipe and chimney were at an unusual angle when I went to check out the damage. God only knew where Ricky holed up and Bonnie worried he might be hurt. Greg, old enough to have lived through one other storm like this one, took it all in stride. He said that the monstrosity of the pier had insulted the water and the water had to have its revenge upon it.

5

RICKY

───────

Autumn was short. After the wind and rain of *Hurricane Grace*, few leaves were left on the trees to change color. The skeleton birches at Francis Point retreated into themselves. By early October, frost had helped itself to anything growing in the community garden. Bonnie and I dug potatoes, carrots and beets and turned them into stews. We ate fish chowders and dreamed of deer and moose stew. We waited for the hunt to begin.

The wreckage of the LNG pier spread out on the shore. No one wanted any part of it. It was just plain bad luck. Eventually the tide would carry it away. The project for LNG to rebuild is on hold. The Oklahoma company that leased our land quit paying the rent and the tribe is out another $40,000 a month on what was to be a twenty-year lease. Piles of firewood appeared in dooryards waiting to be split and stacked; food for hungry wood stoves. Broken down Indian cars and old pickups stood watch. Per capita income completely dried up. The tribe was broke. With the cost of gas at close to four dollars a gallon, people walked the rez instead of driving. Unemployment even in Eastport had risen to seventy-five percent.

People in Hollywood turned off their oil furnaces and cut holes in their roofs to install chimneys for wood stoves. Bonnie didn't want to live alone with winter coming and she prayed that Ricky would come home to help her out. She still refused to put out a missing persons alert on him. If he was using drugs, as she suspected, she didn't want to contribute in any way to his possible arrest. She didn't want her son ending up in the slammer. Although she didn't know it for fact, she'd heard that Ricky's father had been arrested for dealing drugs and was doing time in the state penitentiary at Thomaston. She didn't want her son to meet his father in jail. So she prayed and asked the spirits to watch over her son. And she waited.

By Halloween all the trees were bare and ice formed along the edges of Mirror Lake. The deer hunt would begin on November 1st; on Indian land the moose hunt was well under way. Compared to deer, moose are easy prey. I used to kid around with Peg about how she would seduce the moose to her when she hunted. Peg used a birch bark "moose horn" to call them to her. The bull moose, thinking the call was from a cow in heat, would follow the sound. When it got close enough to her, Peg would take aim and take its life. Now that Peg is gone, we hope that another hunter will share meat with us.

That Halloween I decided to go over to Bonnie's to help her hand out goodies. We chose bags of popcorn and tootsie rolls to offer to the trick-or-treaters. Every kid on the rez made their way through Hollywood on the night of Halloween. Even some adults dressed in costumes. We looked forward to ghosts and goblins knocking at the door.

Luckily Bonnie owned an electric popcorn popper. We spent the afternoon popping corn and filling brown paper lunch bags. I walked over to the Super Saver and bought all the tootsie rolls they had on the shelf. Back at Bonnie's, I put them in a large mixing bowl. We were ready for the onslaught. "Bring it on!" Bonnie said with a wide grin.

As soon as the sun set, kids started knocking: ugly witches and fairy princesses, white-sheeted ghosts and batmen, spider men and even sister and brother pumpkins. But ninjas and SpongeBobs ruled the night along with a pair of nine-year-old twins dressed as salt and pepper. By 8:30, the popcorn was gone. The tootsie rolls disappeared much earlier, despite my attempt at enforcing the one-per-person rule. Around nine I was ready to go home and feed my wood stove, but there was a knock at Bonnie's door and it didn't sound like a kid's knock. We looked at each other as if to say, "You go," but since it was Bonnie's house I stepped back.

When the door opened I heard, "Oh my God," before I could see who is there. In walks Ricky. He is wearing a red-and-black wool hunting jacket and has the hood pulled over his head. He has grown taller and looks down at Bonnie with a wide grin.

"Hi Mom."

"Is that you son?"

"Yup it's me," he says bending down to hug her.

Ricky turns and greets me, "Hi Dous. How's it going?"

"Goin' good."

Ricky has become a man. His long dark brown hair is tied back in a braid that reaches to his waist. Under his jacket he wears a red sweat shirt with *SKIN* printed on the chest. His jeans are clean and the cuffs rolled up over leather winter boots that look brand new. He is broad shouldered and looks much healthier than he did in August. When he takes off his gloves, I notice a small tattoo on his left wrist. One ear is pierced and he wears a small gold hoop in it.

His green eyes shine in the dim light of Bonnie's living room.

"Still fishin'?" I ask.

"No more," he answers. "It's hunting season."

"Well, I'd better get home before my fire goes out," I say reaching for my jacket and heading for the door. "See you guys later."

Ricky moved back in with Bonnie, but he refused to sleep in his old bedroom at the back of the trailer. He preferred to sleep on the living room couch. Evidently, he came home with some cash because the first thing he did was buy a wood stove and cut a hole in the living room roof to install a chimney. Then he bought four cords of eight-foot firewood and a chain saw, axe, and sledge. He had his work cut out for him. Ricky refused to socialize on the rez. He told Bonnie he didn't trust anyone there.

"You grew up with these folks," Bonnie told him.

"That's right," he said. "I grew up."

He didn't even go into Eastport to the Lobster Pot Bar. He was of age to drink but evidently he didn't. Bonnie backed off. She was content that he had returned and that he was preparing the trailer for winter and he had money that he was willing to share. Ricky spent his days cutting and splitting firewood. In the evenings, he watched TV until he fell asleep. Most of the time the TV was left on until Bonnie got up in the night to use the bathroom and turned it off.

One such night about a month after Rick returned, Bonnie got up as usual and went in to turn off the TV. Ricky was gone. His blankets neatly folded on the couch. She looked around for a note but saw nothing, then she went to the door and opened it. The frigid night air slapped her face. She decided against getting dressed and going outside to look for Ricky. Instead, she closed the door, turned the dead bolt, and retreated to her bedroom.

Ricky walks the highway off the rez into the black night. Thick low clouds hug the shore. A full moon struggles to light the night but leaves only a hazy glow in its place in the sky. No cars pass. He stuffs his frozen hands into his jacket pockets. Ricky walks through Chibesquiog (the swamp), a low lying area where people often see the old ones. Some people call them ghosts, others say they are spirits who can't find their way to the other side. Ricky had heard the stories but he didn't believe them. He called them "crazy superstitions."

It is only a short distance to a pay phone outside the WAB. He steps inside the booth and makes a call. Then he waits. No one is around. The damp cold settles into his bones and he shivers. Wind blows against the thin walls of the phone booth. A heavy wet snow begins to fall. It clings to trees and lays down on the ground. Soon the letters on the sign for the Wabanaki Café are illegible. No cars pass.

"Jesus," he mutters. "I'll be trapped here in a whiteout." He lights a cigarette and takes a long drag. The red tip glows in the dark. Why hadn't he remembered to carry a flashlight? Just as he was beginning to let go of all hope of being found, he saw headlights in the distant blowing snow. In just a few minutes, a red Chevy pickup pulled up to the phone booth and stopped.

"Get in!" Simon shouted.

"Am I glad to see you. What's the drivin' like?"

"Here, I'll slide over and you try."

"We need a load in the back to get some traction."

"Would help if your tires weren't bald," Ricky said, holding tight to the steering wheel.

"OK Mr. Money bags, you buy some tires," Simon retorts. He is in a foul mood.

They drive slowly, very slowly, down Route 1 towards Machias. The snow continues to fall heavily. No snow plows clear the road. The two lane highway is one wide snow path and they are the ones making the path. Luckily, no one else is crazy enough to be out driving in this storm. Ricky holds tight to the steering wheel, but he can't see where he is driving in zero visibility. He downshifts into second gear at the bottom of the long hill leading into Pembroke. There are no gas stations, no places to pull over. He is afraid if he does pull off the road, he will never get back on it. If they can make it to Machias, there is a motel where they can get out of the storm. That is, if they can make it to Machias.

The road from Pembroke to Machias, even in good weather, is a desolate stretch of highway lined by a forest of tall balsam fir and ancient pine trees. At Whiting, they will have to drive through the blueberry barrens, a long stretch of open fields. Surely, the blizzard wind will blow them off the road. "Where the hell are we?" Simon asks.

"Damned if I know," Ricky answers. "We've just got to keep truckin' 'til we get to Machias."

They drive on. Hours pass. The light changes from black night to the blue gray of sunrise. The snow does not let up. The wind roars out of the northeast and the truck creeps along, heater blasting.

"Did you make the connection?" Ricky asks.

"Yeah, the plan is to meet at Helen's Restaurant tomorrow around five pm. The place will be busy then. You won't stand out on a Friday night when every Tom, Dick, and Harry is out for the fish fry special."

"Where's he from? Portland? Boston?"

"Hell if I know, he just said he would drive down the coast and meet us at Helen's." Simon is clearly annoyed. He had not expected weather to complicate this deal.

"Sounds good."

The snow falls in sidewise sheets. This blizzard is not ready to give up. Hours later the sky brightens. Sunrise casts an eerie light over the land. They pass a visible road sign that reads: *Machias 3 miles*. They are almost there! At Machias, they pulled into the Downeaster Motel. Exhausted, they crashed on the lumpy motel beds and travel into their dreams. At three in the afternoon Ricky opens his eyes.

"I'm starving!"

"Me, too," Simon responds. "Let's take a shower and get something to eat. Then I split. What's the weather?"

Ricky pulled open the curtains. The snow had stopped. "Sunny but cold," he answers. By the time Ricky reached Helen's restaurant it was 5:15 pm. Simon had vanished and Ricky was on his own.

The restaurant was crowded. Mostly families out for Friday night fish dinner filled the wooden booths with red vinyl seats. "Wall to wall Whities," Ricky muttered. He is so used to hanging out with Indians, he feels like he is on another planet. Simon told him to look for a middle-aged black man with a beard wearing a navy peacoat. He would also be wearing a white shirt and a red tie. African-Americans are very scarce in this part of the country; he knew he'd find the man.

A blond waitress with a red bow mouth greets Ricky. "One tonight?" she asked.

"No, I'm meeting someone, can I have a look around?"

"Sure, go right ahead," she said, her long hair swung like a tail down her back as she led Ricky into the dining room. The aroma of fish chowders and hot biscuits made him hungry all over again but he was nerved up. This was a big deal. He'd eat after. He was wearing his vest anyhow and he knew he wouldn't be able to eat. "What's your friend look like?" the waitress asked.

"A tall black man," he answers.

"Oh! He's right here." She pointed to a booth by a window overlooking the Machias River. There he sat looking out the window, a lone black man in Machias, Maine. He is clean shaven and does not wear a tie. Instead he wears a red flannel shirt and jeans. Ricky approached the booth. "Hi! I'm Rick. Simon sent me."

"Oh good. Sit down," the black man said with

a flashing smile. "Can I buy you a cup of chowder?"

"No thanks, I just want to get down to business."

"That's fine," the black man replied, pushing aside his plate of fried haddock and french fries.

"How should we do this?"

"What are you driving?" Ricky asked.

"A black Chevy Camaro with Massachusetts plates. It's parked in the lot over by the sign for this place. You know the one that says: *Best Homemade Pies in the USA.*"

"OK. Give me the keys and I'll meet you out there in ten minutes. Just pay your bill and walk out casually. You might want to stop at the gift shop and pick up a down Maine souvenir on your way out." Ricky gave orders now. He surprised himself by his self-confident tone of voice. Inside he was shaking.

It was dark but Ricky found the car easily. He unlocked the door on the passenger side and got in. He slipped off his woolen jacket and unbuttoned his flannel shirt. He wore a white smuggler's vest against his skin. Its pockets were full of cocaine, $50,000 worth. He slowly removed the vest, then put on his shirt. As he was buttoning it, the black man knocked on the driver's side window. He unlocked the door and let him in. "Where's the cash?" Ricky asks.

"Right here in this briefcase," the black man says. "It's in $100 bills. You can count them if you want to."

Ricky opens the briefcase and sees the money. He thumbs through the bills to estimate the amount. Five piles of $100 bills, one hundred bills per pile. He had never seen this amount of money. His heart races.

"That looks right. Here's the dope. Let's call it a done deal. Could you drop me off at the Hertz rental car place on the way out of town?" He was in a hurry to get back on the road.

"Sure, no problem."

Ricky rented a blue Ford hatchback and headed home. It is an easy drive back to the rez. He would be home in time to watch *CSI*, he thought. The highway was clear despite four-foot snow banks on the roadsides. Driving was easy after the crawl he made to Machias twenty-four hours ago. He was happy to race home. But when he got to Perry, a small town bordering the reservation, his troubles began.

There is a four-way stop in Perry, just before you reach the WAB and Indian land. Ricky barreled through the stop at sixty miles per hour. He just wasn't thinking. Or rather he was thinking, but of the wrong things: what he would tell Bonnie about his overnight disappearance, where he would take her out to celebrate, where he would stash the $50,000 for safe keeping, what kind of vehicle he would buy them to have reliable transportation for a change? He didn't see the state police car parked at the four way stop. Not until he noticed flashing lights in his rear view mirror and he heard the sirens. He had to think quick. He could stop and risk arrest or make a run for tribal land where the state police had no jurisdiction. He decided to run.

Ricky pressed the gas pedal to the floor. The odometer hit 75 mph, 85 mph, then 90 mph. It was dark; he turned off his head lights. He knew his way home. The clock on the dash read 8:30 pm. Bingo would be getting out soon at St.

Anne's parish hall. He'd park behind the church, disappear into the crowd.

The ghosts of Chibesquiog watched the unfamiliar blue car slice through the night. Better slow down now, he thought, lifting his foot from the gas pedal. He passed the turn to Hollywood and headed across the highway to the red brick church. The Jesuits had come here in the 1600s to set up a mission and save Indian souls. No priest had lived here for many years. The church was used for weddings, funerals and Bingo. Ricky downshifted as he approached the church. He pulled into the parking lot behind the church. Tonight, the parish hall would be filled with bingo players. It's Triple Your Fun Friday. Buy One Get One Free! Soon the bingo players would pour out of the church.

Ricky pulled to the back of the church and parked. A full moon rose out of the bay, vanished behind a bank of clouds then reappeared. By its light everything was revealed. In its darkness all was hidden. Sitting in his rental car with $50,000 dollars, Ricky wished that he could control the movement of the moon. In her darkness he would travel house to house throughout the village. At each house he would leave $100 bills. Under doors, in mailboxes, under windshield wipers of battered pickups, he would accomplish his giveaway. In the moon's darkness he'd visit old Gregory. He wouldn't chance Greg's blindness to find the money, so he would enter and put the money under his tea cup on his table. Greg never locked his door. In Hollywood he'd hide the money in pockets of clothes left in cars and hanging by doors. He'd walk through Chibesquiog and throw one hundred dollar bills to the ghosts who lived there. He would sing them honoring songs and they would recognize him by his Indian name. He would ask their forgiveness for refusing to look at them in his dreams. At the WAB, he'd fill the tip jar on Eddie Francis's counter. He'd stop by the Elderly Center and leave money placed in envelopes under the doors of each tiny apartment. There'd be enough for Bingo Bucks for the rest of their lives.

When he was finished, Ricky would return to Bonnie's trailer and move back into his old bedroom where he could watch the sun and the moonrise out of the bay. He would know that he was a good hearted man.

6

THE GHOSTS OF CHIBESQUIOG

The bear is ravenous. She carries her head low to the ground, shoulders humped. She moves with determination and slowly lumbers out of the forest. She has slept away winter. Scratching an ancient pine tree, she tears the skin from the tree and stuffs the bark into her gaping mouth. Her immense appetite rules every movement. She must eat. Snow covers the land. The she-bear stops at a dumpster outside the tribal café where she finds fish heads and table scraps. She devours everything but her hunger persists.

The bear walks the highway towards the reservation and enters the swamp at Chibesquiog. Willows have begun to green but ice still hardens the land. Shoots have pushed themselves through the ice. Red stems turned yellow then green, warmed by the springtime sun. She bends and twists the willow withies until she is able to feed herself.

The ghosts of Chibesquiog watch the bear gorge herself as she moves among them. They know physical need has forced her to enter the swamp. In the swamp there is no confusion between the living and the dead. Only the dead reside in Chibesquiog. But the bear has survived the long winter only because her body absorbed the two fetus cubs she had carried into the den. Too emaciated to feed them into birth, her body took them back into itself.

At six am, Bonnie wakes with a splitting headache. She stumbles into her tiny kitchen and pushes the ON button of her coffeemaker. My dream is still with me, she tells herself. Why would I enter the swamp at Chibesquiog, she wonders.

No one goes there. We all know it is a haunted place. Even old Greg refuses to look at the place when we drive by. He finds an excuse to cover his eyes even though he is mostly blind. There is no way in or out of the reservation without passing the haunted swamp. Now Bonnie remembers that the tribal council is discussing the possibility of filling in this wetland and building HUD houses there. But are they crazy? No one will ever want to live there.

In Bonnie's dream there are houses there. Not the usual poorly built HUD houses, but sturdy log homes with stone fireplaces and bay windows facing the sea. And there are trees growing there: tall maples, ash and oak, old growth like the ones that have disappeared from the reservation now. There were trees growing in the old days but over the years they were cut for firewood.

Bonnie fixes her coffee and returns to her

bed. Her headache lightens as the caffeine goes to her head. Why would they build at Chibesquiog when they know that restless spirits have owned that place for as long as anyone can remember? Its inhabitants are those who, for one reason or another, had trouble making it to the other side; those who suicided or killed someone in a rage or were killed by someone or even those whose families refused to let them go refused to let them make their journey to the other side. Her dream began to float away. She could not remember why or how the houses were built there or who lived in them.

Bonnie's health is not improving. There are days when she doesn't leave her bed. Her doctors have no answers, even with one test after another. At least once a month she makes the long trip to Bangor to the medical center but she comes home drained, depressed, and exhausted. Bonnie prays for answers and for her health to return, but she has a deep-seated fear in her gut that she will not get well again. There are days when she is unable to walk. Dizzy spells plague her and make her afraid to leave her home. She has fallen a few times. There are times when she is unable to eat and she has lost twenty pounds in the last few months. She fears these are her last days and she will leave this earth without even knowing what or who killed her.

The phone by her bed rings. "Hello, Dous is that you?" Her life-long friend calls this time every day to check on her.

"How's it going today?" Dous asked.

"Not so good. I'm having trouble walking again and the last few nights I've had these strange dreams."

"What dreams?"

"Well, maybe if I talk about them, I'll chase them away." Bonnie sighs. She sets down her coffee cup and lights a cigarette inhaling deeply. "Have you heard anything about them building houses at Chibesqiuog?" Bonnie asked Dous.

"Well, there was something about it in the tribal newsletter last week. Something about a big Bingo hall and maybe a casino and resort cabins too. But you know the tribe is broke," Dous replied.

"That doesn't matter. One of those fat cat backers from Harrah's would finance the whole thing in a minute if they thought they could make a buck." Bonnie puts out her cigarette and limps into her kitchen.

"Well, it could happen, there are no casinos within 300 miles from here and we all know that Indians love to gamble, and white people, too."

"But everybody's poor here," Bonnie protests. She is still trying to chase the dreams away.

"That's alright," Dous told her. "They'll bus tourists in from Canada and Bangor and even the south if the stakes are good enough and then they'll even build a hotel. Just like in Connecticut. Look what the Pequots did."

A light flashes in Bonnie's mind, "That's where the log cabins came from."

"What log cabins?" Dous asked.

"In my dream," Bonnie said. "There were these big log cabins with stone fireplaces and windows looking out onto the bay."

"That would create some action around here. There would be a real nightlife."

"And some jobs, too. Maybe even I could get work," Bonnie suddenly was excited by the idea, forgetting everything she knew about gambling and addictions.

"Me too," Dous replied with a half laugh. "They are supposed to bring it up at the council meeting tomorrow night. Want to go see what's cooking?"

"Yeah, let's do it."

Dous hangs up the phone and thinks back to the days when she and Bonnie were growing up together at Northpoint. We've always been close, she remembers. We went to high school together until Bon had to drop out to give birth to her son Ricky. I never wanted to have kids. I thought the guys around there were so irresponsible they leave you barefoot and pregnant while they gypsy around and don't answer to anyone. Look at my own father; he just took off leaving my mother six months pregnant and saying he couldn't hack reservation life. We never heard from him after that. Not a word, no checks, nothing. I've never met him. Still haven't.

"Anyhow, Bon and I are close," Dous mumbles to herself. "We watch out for each other." Like the time I decided to run for governor. It caused such an uproar for a woman to run for tribal office. Some jerk put a homemade pipe bomb in my old Toyota. Bonnie got wind of it and warned me, otherwise I would have been blown to smithereens when I started the car. But I'm not bitter about that; I just wish I could find work around here. I'm tired of collecting general assistance. GA doesn't give you enough to get by on, let alone save. I'd like to save some money to get plumbing hooked up to my cabin. It gets damn chilly in the outhouse once winter sets in.

Bonnie sleeps most of the day. She tries to get back to her dream of resort cabins and the casino at Chibesquiog but has no luck.

The next day at 5:30 pm, Dous appears at Bonnie's door. "Ready for the council meeting?" she asks as she walks into the trailer.

There is no answer. "Hey Bon, are you ready to go?" Dous asks in a louder voice. Still no answer.

Dous walks through the kitchen to the back of the trailer. Silence. Her heart races as her mind thinks the worst. Bonnie's bedroom door is closed. She knocks and then she gently opens the door. Bonnie's bed is neatly made with her blinds open. Warm sunshine spills into the room. On the night stand near her bed is an unopened pack of Marlboro Lights and an empty coffee mug. There is also a hand written note of two words: GONE WALKING.

Dous is stunned. "Walking! Where?" she mutters. "She can barely get around her house with a cane! How the hell can she go walking?" Dous picks up the phone to call tribal police.

"Anybody seen Bonnie Neptune walking around?" she asks.

"Nobody has called. You want to report her missing?" dispatch asks.

"Oh Hell, I don't even know how long she's been gone. Maybe we should wait a while but you know she doesn't get around very well. She can barely walk these days."

"OK then, call back if you want."

Dous hangs up the phone and decides to drive around the rez to look for Bonnie. She drives the dirt road out of Hollywood onto the highway. Maybe Bonnie decided to go up to the WAB for cigarettes, she thinks, before she remembers the unopened pack of Marlboros on her night stand. She drives on anyway, on the chance that someone there has seen her. The evening light softens the harsh reality of Bonnie's disappearance. It is low tide. Seabirds linger along the shore. Seagulls and cormorants trail a fishing boat making its way between First Island and Second Island headed for the pier at Eastport. Dous drives towards Chibesquiog. She wonders what is pulling her in that direction but a gut feeling overcomes rational thought. "Why would she go there?" She asks herself.

The sun drops into the bay and the temperature sinks. It's going to freeze again tonight Dous tells herself. She down shifts into second gear as she approaches the low land of Chibesquiog. In the fading light she sees a figure walking out of the swamp. Her first thought, "Bear," she murmurs as the dark figure slowly approaches the highway. But as she draws closer, she realizes that the bear has long hair and wears a dark overcoat.

"Oh My God! It's Bonnie," she yells. "But where is her cane?"

Dous stops the truck and gets out. Bonnie's

bloodied face is covered with scratches. An arm of her coat is torn away at the shoulder and her jeans are ripped at her knees. When Dous questions her, Bonnie refuses to speak. But she does crawl into the pickup.

"Want to go to the health center?" Dous asks, looking her over. Bonnie shakes her head no.

"Home, then?" Dous asks, still staring.

Bonnie shakes a yes and they drive to her trailer. Bonnie sleeps for two days straight. There is no waking her. Dous stayed with her the first night and watched her toss and turn and groan until she herself fell asleep. The next day she left. She needed answers, so she decided to visit Greg, the oldest tribal member. When he was younger he fished the treacherous waters of the Passamaqoddy Bay in a canoe. He tells stories of times when there were so many fish people went to the shore and scooped them up with bare hands. Greg is mostly blind now. He rarely leaves his home and lives in his visions. He still has a head of thick white hair and wears glasses that are magnifiers. Although his eyesight is bad, his hearing is still very acute. He hears the whales when they enter the bay and he goes to the shore to listen to their songs.

Dous walks over to Greg's house less than a quarter mile from her home. She enters without knocking which is the custom among close friends and tribal members. She tells Greg what happened to Bonnie and asks for his advice. He closes his eyes for a few minutes and then tells her to ask the bear.

"What bear?" she replies, annoyed at his answer.

"The bear that's been roaming this reservation for weeks," he answers. "Didn't you hear? It was seen near Chibesquiog. It even broke into Bob Cat's fish house and ate a barrel of alewives and herring he was using to bait his traps. A whole barrel! That bear must have had a wicked case of diarrhea after that," Greg chuckled.

"Greg, this is no laughing matter," Dous scolds. "Bonnie could have been killed but unless I'm way off track, she's been healed."

"Healed?" Greg asks.

"She walked out of that swamp standing tall with no limp and no cane."

"We'll see," Greg seems surprised. "See how she is when she wakes up." Time will tell."

"I'd better get back over there now. Have to stop by my place for clean clothes. I'll keep you posted."

Greg stared out his bay window, like he did everyday. Sitting at his wooden table sipping Lipton tea with sugar and milk in his blue enamel cup.

Dous leaves Greg's warm kitchen and walks back out into the sunny cold day. At her own cabin she picks up a change of clothes. Then she gets in her pickup and drives to the Super Saver for groceries. She had noticed that the refrigerator at Bonnie's was empty. When Bonnie does wake up, she'll probably be famished, she thinks.

Driving through Chibesquiog, she thinks of the bear. Had Bonnie been mauled by the bear, or healed, or both? Greg told her that time would tell but she wanted answers. Dous knows bears are healers. She knows this from her clan stories and what she has heard all her life from the elders. But she knows that bears can also be fierce killers. She knew a story about a she-bear that lived in Chibesquiog and would only show herself to women. Dous wonders if Bonnie encountered that same bear. When Bonnie was up for talking she would ask her about the bear.

A year passes. Bonnie's hair grays and her former easy laughter comes harder now. But she seems calmer and she can walk without a cane. She doesn't mention her old pains. And she never speaks about her experience at Chibesquiog or the bear. No one dares to ask. Dous knows better than to pry. She is just very happy that her old friend can walk again.

7

BINGO MANIA

———

The tribe makes a deal with Harrah's, for an enormous bingo hall to be erected on tribal land at the edge of Chibesquiog. State regulations forbids Indians to build casinos off reservation. The residents of Maine voted in referendums several times against Indian gaming enterprises off reservation, but on tribal land the state has no jurisdiction.

"If we build it, they will come!" supporters tell those opposed to the venture.

"There'll be jobs for everyone and a hefty per capita income to be enjoyed by tribal members," supporters tell the people of Northpoint.

There is no referendum vote by the tribal membership. The tribal council meets, they vote in favor. That's that. Then we watch thickly forested tribal land in the western part of the state that was acquired after the land claims settlement in the 1970's, as well as thousands of acres of blueberry lands, put up as collateral. Harrah's backs and finances the money to build.

The first building to go up on the reservation is a giant bingo hall. It's nothing like Bonnie's dream of a plush resort. Just a quonset hut type building with no windows but it can accommodate five hundred players. It's a start. And many tribal members are excited about it.

Bingo is on Friday and Saturday nights with a half price matinee on Saturday afternoons. St. Anne's church bingo folds but no one cares. The stakes are higher now and jobs are there for those who want them. Tribal members are supposed to have hiring preference but given the high unemployment in the area people come from as far away as Machias to apply. Even some Canadians who live on the other side of the bridge from Calais are convinced that they can get working papers if a job is offered.

But for now the bingo hall only offers a limited number of jobs. Eddie Francis, the cook at the Wabanaki Café decides to open his own concession in the bingo hall and hire a few people to help. The menu will be limited but with hundreds expected, he's sure he can make a killing selling hot dogs, mooseburgers, chips and Cokes. He has an idea to try Frito pies as well. He'd learned about them when his wife Alice made them for supper one night. Alice attended the Indian Art Institute in Santa Fe, New Mexico, years ago and remembered the recipe: Fritos, chili beans, shredded cheese with lettuce, tomatoes, and onions. He was sure they'd be a big hit if he didn't make the chili too hot. Everyone loves beans.

There is one job as a bingo caller and a few positions as floor clerks to sell specials and pay the winners. They also need a few cashiers to sell daubers, the paper packs, and to arrange for payouts. Eventually they hope to go to electronic machines, but for starters they will keep it low tech and use paper.

The manager or "Bingo Boss" as she is called, is appointed by the tribal council. Their choice was Molly Paul, a known and experienced bingo nut who has frequented the high stakes games run by the Penobscots for years. People joked that she should know how to run a bingo joint since she has spent half of her life in one. And then too, she is also the niece of a long term council member.

Molly is pushing sixty-years-old, with jet black dyed hair showing her white around the edges and at the roots. She wears thick horned rimmed glasses most of the time on the tip of her nose. Her black deep set eyes peer straight into the mind of anyone who foolishly tries to deceive her. Her eyes are the kind that take but do not give. People say Molly is a mind reader and you'd better watch your thoughts around her. She can take them if she wants them.

But before the Bingo Palace opens, comes the rain. Rain and fog for thirty-nine days straight, all of June and into July. Everything molds.

Even people start to take on a greenish tinge. The temperature never rises out of the 50's. The seed potatoes rot in their furrows at the community garden. Bees trucked in from North Carolina to pollinate the blueberry fields remain in their hives. Even if they could fly, which bees refuse to do in rain, with all the water and no sun, no flowers form on the blueberry bushes for them to pollinate. By early July, when the sun finally pokes through the thick fog, the bees with a wicked sense of cabin fever swarm, and they swarm again. No one tries to catch the swarms. The bees go feral.

Molly Paul seems to have foreseen this long-term spell of inclement weather. She takes a few weeks off and travels to Albuquerque, New Mexico, to visit friends. "Call me when it stops raining," she tells her uncle. He does and when she returns to Northpoint, she has a tan and a taste for New Mexico green chili. "We've got to have green chili mooseburgers on the menu," she tells Eddie Francis.

"OK, but where do we get the chili?" he asks.

"I've got friends," Molly answers in a huff, bossy as usual.

After the rains, Molly convinces the tribal council that the bingo hall should have a grand opening with a Saturday half-priced matinee, followed by a full-priced Saturday night Bonanza on the July 4th weekend. They go along with her plan and Northpoint Bingo Palace is born in the big quonset hut. Of course the tour buses roll in from Bangor, St. Stephen, New Brunswick, and Portland to play, but it is our own Northpoint pride and people who fill the hall. Every tribal member is given a free six card paper pack for the twenty-two games and specials are half price. Daubers, used to block out numbers on the cards, are on the house for the first 200 customers.

My friend Bonnie is generally opposed to gambling, but she goes along with the opening celebration. Anyway, she has her eye on the brand new Toyota Tacoma 4×4 pickup that will be raffled off on Sunday night and she wants to accumulate as many tickets as possible for chances to win. I agree to pick her up early so we can stake out our spot. The doors open at 11:30 am. Early Bird specials start at 12:30 pm.

Bonnie finds a lucky spot: at the fourth long

table, fourth chair over on the north side. Her hearing is not as good as it used to be and she needs a clear view of the overhead TV screen to see the bingo balls just in case the caller mumbles. The hall is nosy and there is a a lot of commotion with people setting up their places putting down their lucky charms and getting situated. Bonnie just sits and says a little prayer for luck.

New to bingo, she's happy to see the three Francis sisters, her mother and two aunts, take seats beside her. They are ladies in their 70's and experienced bingo players. She knows they will offer advice. Her mother Edna Francis tells her to put her purse on the chair between them and to leave it open just a little so money can flow inside. Edna works fifteen cards at a time and Bonnie is sure Edna will tell her if she misses a number.

I, on the other hand, decide not to play. I want to check the place out and see who is doing what. I can really use a job and I think maybe there's a place for me in the bingo hall. Secretly, I have wanted for a long time to be a bingo caller. The idea of so many people hanging on my every word, or number, gives me the feeling of a tremendous sense of power.

I am built big-boned and solid. Not fat, mind you, just solid. My long dark braid hangs nearly to my waist and my wide smile has a way of drawing people to me, even if I do say so myself. Everyone greets me. I station myself near Eddie's concession stand and not far from the podium where the numbers are called.

Molly had already hired her most current boyfriend, Jimmy Shay to call. Jim is a Penobscot but has lived on this rez ever since he and Molly decided to shack up. Jim is as fair skinned as Molly is dark and is often taken to be a white man. But he's on the Penobscot rolls. Fair skin and light eyes are common among the Penobscots.

Jim opens the games by reading the rules of the house and he begins to call the numbers. But he turns out to be a mumbler, and for the elderly who are hard of hearing, this becomes a problem.

"Did he say B-47 or G-47" Edna asks Bonnie. Looking up she says, "There it is on the TV screen, G-47." Bonnie points with her lips at the number. As the games continue, Jimmy's calling gets worse. When it came to the odd/even game, he is only supposed to call out even numbers since it is the 4th of July. Even days, even numbers; odd days, odd numbers. But Jimmy has trouble telling an odd from an even number and he just calls any number that comes up.

This puts Molly over the edge. "What the hell is going on!" she shouts. "Jimmy get away from that mike! Dous, you take over!"

I am in shock. Much as I have dreamed of calling, I'm not ready. "Who me?" I ask. "Yup, just get up there. We'll talk about pay later but I'll make it worth your while."

So I take the plunge and I do very well. After the tenth game and before the ten-minute intermission and bathroom break, I even get a round of applause. Everything is going along just fine until the eighteenth game, the U Pick Em. That's the game invented where a person writes in numbers 1-75 and hopes the caller calls seven of their numbers in a row. At first the crowd thinks Eddie has left too many hot dogs on the grill and they're burning. But as smoke begins to fill the bingo hall, panic seizes the crowd. I have the microphone and I try to calm things down but it's no use when I also start coughing. Something is burning! People are coughing and scrambling for the door. This is a quonset hut and was built with only one door. A stampede begins.

Molly calls 911 on her cell phone. She screams at dispatch:

"FIRE! FIRE! FIRE IN THE BINGO HALL!"

The nearest fire department is miles away in Eastport and the all-white volunteer crew takes their sweet time driving to the rez. It is a terrible scene. Old ladies and men, some with canes and walkers, are desperate for rescue. Edna Francis becomes disorientated by the smoke and just sits down and begins to recite the rosary. Soon it catches on and pretty soon, "Hail Mary Full of Grace," can be heard amid the coughing and swearing and cries for help. I go back and help Edna outside. Everyone gets out alive but there are many injuries, mostly sprains and bruises in the rush for the door. Molly is hyperventilating so badly. She has to be rushed to Calais Hospital for fear she is having a heart attack. Finally, the fire is put out. A week later the results from an investigation conducted by the fire department investigation shows that a hungry seagull flew into the exhaust fan on Eddie's grill. The bird plugged the exhaust and the fire started. The bird is now cooked. It turns out a sprinkler system was installed but not hooked up to a water source. The fire had its way with the building.

The rest is history. The Northpoint Bingo Paradise is condemned. What's worse, it is cursed. No one will go back into that Quonset hut. It just sits there, the shell of it, like a giant caterpillar waiting to metamorphosize. In late September, St. Anne's Church restarts their basement bingo. The stakes are lower, but people feel secure gambling in a church.

8

REVENGE OF THE SNOOP
SISTERS

Every day the old women walk the rez; Edna, Helen, and Grace Francis, three sisters born and raised at Northpoint. They investigate people and things and keep their secret discoveries to themselves. Northpoint is a small place as Indian reservations go. It covers less than eighty acres and is bounded on three sides by water.

It is located in the far northeastern corner of the state of Maine. All three sisters are in their seventies, born just two years apart from each other. All three are built the same, short and stocky, not fat but padded.

Edna is the oldest of the three. She is fair-skinned and a red head. It is obvious that her father was a white man from Eastport, but she vehemently denies this.

"I had the same damn father as you," she told her sister Grace one day. Grace just looked hard at her and didn't say a word.

Unlike Edna, Grace is dark with olive brown skin and black deep-set eyes. Grace is the quiet one. She has six children living but birthed ten. All of her children have different fathers.

Then there is Helen, the middle sister. Helen and Grace look alike having had the same father but they are very different. Helen is a talker. "She loves to hear the sound of her own voice," is how Edna explains Helen's ability to go on and on about a subject.

It is a cool late autumn day and the Francis "Snoop" Sisters are out for their daily walk. They have been circling the rez on the two dirt roads that surround the village. It is nearly noon and they are approaching the elderly center where they eat most days. Suddenly Helen blurts out, "The bingo hall fire was no accident."

"What do you mean no accident?" Grace asks. "That damn seagull caused the fire. The investigation proved that. It got caught in the exhaust fan from Eddie Francis' grill and started the fire."

"Well that's just not true," Helen shoots back. "I know better."

"Just what *do* you know?" Edna asks.

Now that Helen has her sisters' attention, she has the stage and she plans to savor every moment of it. She walks away towards the elderly center leaving Grace and Edna standing in shock. By now they are talking Indian and she knows she has them hooked. They have never known Helen to lie or make up stories but they also know that this is serious. If the seagull didn't cause the bingo hall fire, then who or what did?

Edna and Grace follow Helen into the elderly meal site. It is a large well lit room with a bay window on the east side facing the ocean. Three long tables covered with floral patterned oilcloths are situated in the middle of the room. To the south is a swinging door which opens into a small kitchen where meals are prepared.

Helen sits at their usual table near the window. Her sisters eye her suspiciously while they wait for their food.

"Who told you that?" Edna attacked Helen with her words.

"Never mind who, I just know what I know," Helen teased.

"Well, why did the Bingo hall burn?" Grace asked.

"You know we can't talk about it here." Helen looks around, "too many ears. Let's just eat."

Grace looks away in disapproval.

Today's menu is baked meatloaf with gravy and mashed potatoes and green beans. A green salad is served on the side but nobody eats it. "Rabbit food," Grace complained. For dessert homemade molasses cake is served with whipped cream, Edna's favorite.

Outside the wind has picked up and the temperature has dropped. Storm clouds are gathering over the bay. "Maybe we should just sit here awhile," Grace told her sisters. "The others will leave and then we can talk."

When the meal site is nearly empty, Grace and Edna give Helen "the look."

"Well?" Edna peers straight through Helen as though she is able to see into her mind. "Who told you about that?" She shoots the words at Helen giving her no choice but to reply.

"Old Greg," Helen shot back.

"What does *he* know? He is blind," Edna scoffed.

"He may be blind but his ears work," Helen defends.

"Well, how did that bingo hall fire get started? Don't forget we all nearly choked to death from the smoke," Edna rolls her eyes and insists her sister explain. "I want the whole story, who what where and when and I want it now."

Helen is enjoying every moment of this drama and she is having trouble keeping a smile from spreading across her face. But she knows her sisters will not relent. They've got her cornered now.

"It was a holy roller," she blurts out unexpectedly.

"Who?" Grace demanded.

"You know one of those damn fools who believe gambling is a mortal sin," Helen whispers. "The Bible thumpers. Eastport is full of them. They got wind that we were having a real big Indian style bingo and they decided to burn us down."

"That's why it took so long for the fire trucks to get here," Grace looks shocked. "They would have just let us cook in there, thinking we'd go straight to hell, anyhow."

"Yup, they would do that," Edna nods and agrees. "Well, we'll fix them. Did Greg tell you who they are?" she asks Helen.

"Nope, he won't give out names," Helen told her. "Says it would just make things worse, but I know he's not making this up."

"Now, how do you know that?" Grace asked.

"A seagull told me," Helen smiles.

"Don't get me wrong. There were warning signs," Helen tells Grace and Edna. "Like the time last summer the congregation of the Church of God in Eastport put on a revival service in their big circus tent and all. They had some screwball minister from down south visit and get everyone all worked up so he could save souls. Remember? His photo was on the front page of the Eastport Times. They quoted him saying, "Even the heathens at Northpoint are welcome to attend our gathering."

"*HEATHENS!* He called us heathens!" Edna shouted. "Oh yes, I remember him now."

"What does he think we do at Mass every Sunday at Saint Anne's? Don't Catholic prayers count?" Grace added.

"Right after he came to Eastport, the next week the 'heathen' community center had a fire, remember?" Helen reminded them, "and no one ever found out how that fire started."

"Well it turns out the investigators were from Eastport volunteer fire department, just like for the bingo hall blaze. Something smells fishy here! We've got to stop this now," Edna stood up raging.

The "Snoop" sisters are united in their efforts to seek revenge for the burnings. Nothing is ever the same after that.

Winter hit early. A nor'easter barreled up the coast from the Carolinas to Maine and left a trail of power outages and snowdrifts in its path.

When the storm hit Northpoint, it was raging both thunder and snow with hurricane force winds. It stalled there before moving up to Nova Scotia and snowed for three days straight. The sisters, needless to say, were unable to take their daily walks.

Not wanting to miss their opportunity to make a plan, Helen and Grace decided to stay over at Edna's. She had the warmest house of the three and plenty of room. They needed time and they needed time together. If it was indeed arson that destroyed their bingo hall, they wanted to get to the root of it. If the fire starters weren't stopped, somebody could get hurt. Helen told them again that Greg refused to disclose the names of the culprits.

"We can bribe him," Edna pipes up over breakfast of oatmeal and toast. She just got off the phone with Bonnie who is her daughter. Bonnie called, checking to see if she is warm and has what she needs during this storm.

"Well, I suppose," Helen answers Edna about a bribe. "But with what? We don't have much money and Greg doesn't really need any, he rarely leaves his home now."

"But he could use a helper," Grace says. "He's always saying he needs a wife."

"At his age!" Edna yells. "He's nothing but a dirty old man."

"All the more reason he'd go for it," Helen chuckled.

Greg has lived alone for most of his eighty-two years. He never married, he had a few shack ups but nothing ever lasted. He said he was just too independent and fishing was his life. "I didn't want anybody worrying and pulling me home when I was out there. A woman would interfere with what I was doing with the fish and the waters." Greg fished from a canoe, because he said a motor would scare the fish away. He never wanted a boat with a motor. He paddled the waters of Passamaquoddy bay when lesser men would haul their rigs and sit at home by the fire. But then Greg grew old. His jet black hair turned white and his eyes clouded. He became like a beached whale. His body was grounded but his heart was still at sea. Now he lived mostly in his visions and memories of the old days.

The storm passes and during its fury a plan

has been made. The sisters are convinced that Greg's secret about the bingo hall fire will be theirs. For a price, of course. Helen was elected to return to Greg with their offer. It made sense since she had already talked with Greg about the fire and besides, the three sisters drew straws and Helen pulled the shortest. Helen insisted she could not go to Greg empty handed so Edna agreed to bake a molasses cake. Helen would deliver it.

Just before noon on the second day after the storm ended, Helen trudged through the snow and appeared at Greg's door. No one knocks at Northpoint. She just opened the door and walked in. Greg is sitting at the table looking out his bay window watching sea smoke rise from the frigid waters.

"Here's a cake for you, old man," Helen tells him placing the cake on the table in front of him. "It's still warm, right out of the oven."

"Well, let's have some then," he tells Helen. "I'll put water on for tea." He does not seem surprised by his visitor. It's as though he had expected her.

Helen sits on a wooden chair facing Greg and

tries to carefully plot her next step. She has clear instructions from Edna and Grace, "Don't come home without the names," they told her when she left them.

Helen and Greg sit silently enjoying the warm cake and Helen waits for the right moment to begin. "Well, I heard the bingo hall fire was set by someone," Helen baits Greg.

"Yup, that's what I was told," Greg answers.

"By who," Helen peers at Greg holding her breath, hoping he'll answer. It should be Edna sitting here, she thinks. She would spook Greg into thinking she could read his mind and then he'd spill the beans.

"It was the Eastport holy rollers. You know how much those damn fools hate Indians." Greg is looking out the window now at storm clouds gathering over the bay. "And to them gambling is a sin."

"Did they have their hands in the community center fire last summer too?" Helen asks.

"Probably. They just want to get rid of us. And I know what I know from a reliable source. Also, you know that they've always wanted this land."

"Well, what can we do to stop them?" Helen asks.

"Poison them," Greg replies offhandedly.

"Poison them like rats?" Helen asks, alarmed at the thought. She didn't like those fanatics, but she wasn't a murderer. "Oh, so we don't have to kill them, just make them sick enough so they will leave us alone." Helen watches his face.

"I've got an idea. I've been thinking about this for a long time now. You want to collaborate?" Greg asks Helen.

"Sure." Greg has Helen's undivided attention now, but she wishes her sisters were with her to hear his plan.

"They are planning one of their Saturday night church suppers next week," Greg tells Helen. "You know it's a potluck except they supply the beans and franks. They are always saying that everyone is invited. Someone told me they put signs up around the rez to invite Indians. I suppose they think if we eat with them, the next thing they'll be praying over us to save our souls."

"I've heard about that," Helen tells Greg. "But would you really want to go over there?"

"Hell no, not me, but you and Edna and Grace could go."

"What would we do there?" Helen asks.

"Just bring your goodies. Two delicious chocolate cakes full of Ex-Lax and a tray or two of marijuana brownies. I've got a special mix for the Kool-Aid punch. When everyone is good and stoned and running to the restroom, I'll call the Eastport cops and they can go bust up the party. You, Grace, and Edna have to high tail it back to the rez before everyone is good and stoned and we all read about it in the *Eastport Times*."

"Well, I'll have to talk with my sisters. I'll get back to you," Helen tells Greg as she puts on her overcoat and walks out the door.

"Is Greg crazy?" She asked herself on the walk home. We get those holy rollers high on marijuana with diarrhea to boot. I wonder what he has in mind for the punch. Helen is chuckling as she walks into Edna's house.

"Well?" Edna greets Helen at the door.

"Call Grace and tell her to get over here right away," Helen said, hanging her coat on a peg by the door. She's still smiling at the thought of Greg's plan. When Grace arrived, the sisters have coffee and Helen tells them what Greg has in mind.

"Where does he get his ideas from?" Grace asks, pulling up a chair for Helen.

"I don't know but our bingo palace is gone and it's easy enough to buy Ex-Lax," Helen said.

"I could get the marijuana from my grandson. I'll just tell Ricky I need it to make some tea for my arthritis. He'll be happy to turn his old grandma into a pothead," Edna says with a chuckle. "And I could ask my grandson to drive us over there and wait for us to drive us back to the rez. We wouldn't have to stay long. I'll just tell him we are bringing food over there for the needy."

"Then Greg would call the cops, an anonymous tip. That would throw them all in the slammer!" Helen said, unable to stop laughing. "I wonder what secret ingredient Greg has in mind for the punch?"

Saturday rolls around. The three sisters spend most of the day baking and laughing. Around 4 pm Helen returns to Greg's to pick up the special Kool-Aid punch. He has it ready in two large gallon jugs. "Now make sure that everyone drinks it. There are no kids at this supper right?"

"No, it's just for the adult church members," Helen told him.

"Now you and Grace and Edna stay away from it," he orders.

"Okay, but what's in it besides Kool-Aid?" Helen asked.

"Oh, just a little secret ingredient that's all."

"Okay, now you call the cops around 6 pm. That should give the Ex-Lax and marijuana time to take effect," Helen tells him as she walks out the door carrying the punch.

Three days later Helen returns to visit Greg with a copy of the *Eastport Times*. The headline reads:

CHURCH OF GOD PARISHIONERS ARRESTED FOR LSD AND MARIJUANA USE
AT SATURDAY NIGHT BEAN SUPPER.
Last Saturday night parishioners at Eastport Church of God were arrested for illegal drug use. They allege that they were unknowingly slipped the

drugs in some food donated at their potluck dinner. "I know it wasn't the beans and franks," a parishioner who wishes to remain anonymous told a Times reporter. "I brought them myself but someone brought food here spiked with Ex-Lax, marijuana and LSD."

When asked if he had any clues as to who would do that he replied, "Three elderly Indian ladies from Northpoint dropped off a delicious chocolate cake and brownies, but we'll never know if it was them because the sweets disappeared in no time. Come to think of it, so did the ladies. The Eastport police have no jurisdiction over at Northpoint. There will be no investigation. This will never be solved. All we know is those drugs left us with a wicked case of diarrhea."

9

WE HAVE TO TALK

———————

Winter returned late that year to the reservation. Maybe it was because of all the rain that fell through the summer, thirty-nine days straight of rain and fog. Snow didn't arrive until late October. It came on heavy just in time for hunting season. Three feet of snow fell in the first storm. Roads were closed, then opened with six-foot-high banks on the sides of the roads made by the snow plows. I ended up in one on my way to Machias and thank God for the snow, otherwise I would have hit a telephone pole. We didn't see bare ground for eight months.

That was the year that Molly Paul called Father Francis Sullivan back to the reservation. "Father Sully," as he was called, had served as pastor for St. Anne's parish ten years ago until he was told by the bishop that he was transferred. It was rumored that he was sleeping with a woman of the parish. But that was over ten years ago and people forget, or at least those with long memories pretend to forget.

After the bingo hall burned down, Molly felt the community needed a cleansing and only Fr. Sully could do it. He is a charismatic priest and some say he has a healing touch. One cold winter morning, Molly crawled out of bed and stumbled into her tiny kitchen. Her boyfriend Jimmy had made coffee before he left for work at the lumberyard in Robbinston. He had left a note with hot coffee and the wood stove filled.

She poured herself a cup of coffee, added sugar, and sat down at her small wooden table. The phone was in its cradle on the wall. She needed to collect her thoughts before making the call. Father Sully and Molly had been very close, too close in fact. Molly wasn't much of a churchgoer but when Sully came to the rez with his compelling smile and red Irish hair, Molly couldn't resist him. He wasn't like the other old priests that had been sent to this remote reservation to save souls. Sully was different. Some made fun of his Irish brogue, others loved him. But would he agree to visit? Could she even find him? Last she heard he was sent to a parish north of Boston, with an Irish and Italian congregation. She wondered how he behaved there? If there had been more sexual indiscretions? Was he still even a priest? Finally, Molly put down her coffee cup and walked to the phone. She had a Massachusetts number, the last number she was given for Sully when he was transferred to St. Mary's Star of the Sea Parish. She decided to give it a try and slowly dialed the 978 area code, then the seven digit number. The phone only rang once.

"Hallo! Father Sullivan here," a loud voice responded.

"That you Sully? It's me, Molly Paul. Do you remember me?"

"Lord in Heaven, Molly Paul. How are you?" the priest asked.

"We have to talk." Molly blurted out the words like tiny bird shot scattering to find its prey.

"Of course, but what's wrong? You don't sound like your cheerful self."

"Cheerful, I never was. Do you know who you are talking to? Molly, Molly Paul, Northpoint reservation, down Maine." Molly is annoyed.

"Yes, of course I remember you Molly. Now what is going on?"

"We need you down here Father. This place is in need of a big time healing. Can you come down? We need a healing Mass."

The priest paused. "Well, let me check my calendar."

Molly thought, he never kept a calendar when he lived with us. Must be a lot more souls down there he is trying to save.

"How soon do you need me?" Sully asked.

"Yesterday," Molly shot back.

"Well, who is the pastor of St. Anne's now?"

"No one. The priest from Eastport comes on Sunday morning to hear confessions and say the ten o'clock Mass. That's it."

"Well then, I guess the church is available." Sully was surprised that no one had filled his shoes after he departed. But given the financial state of the Catholic church after paying lawsuit after lawsuit on behalf of perpetrator priests, he knew it was unlikely that the bishop would spend the money to send another priest to this remote Indian reservation.

Molly grew impatient, "When can you come? We are all yours."

"I'm not sure I'm the man for you." The priest decided to test Molly's intent.

"Yup, you are the one. There's trouble here and only you will know what to do."

"I'll have to think this over. I'll call you in a few days." The priest hung up.

Molly is furious. How dare Sully cut her off like that after all they had been through. She immediately redialed the number. No answer. Molly is a woman who gets her way at all costs and she knows how to get Sully's attention.

She'd just give him a day or two, she thought. If he doesn't call back, she'll call him and tell him, "We need a confessor." Sully did tend to be a busy body and he liked to know every person's business. He would not be able to resist the opportunity to catch up on the latest events at Northpoint Reservation.

The following weekend Sully returned to Northpoint. When he arrived, he decided right away to hear confessions before the evening Mass. Of course Molly was the first person in the confessional. "Bless me Father for I have sinned. It has been a very long time since my last confession. I don't even remember just how long."

"What are your sins?" Sully asked sitting on the other side of the dark curtain.

"Well, I have a lot of little sins and one big one." She knew how to engage his interest.

"Let's hear the big one first," the priest told her. He was curious about what Molly had been up to since he left. Who she was sleeping with, etc.

"I had a child. Father did you know you are a father?"

"What? What did you say?" Sully tried to catch his breath, he is shocked.

"I said YOU fathered my child." Molly begins to cry but quickly composes herself.

"What, I what?" Sully is whispering now.

"You know our secret meetings from years ago when you lived here. How we carried on. Don't tell me you forgot." Molly can feel her anger rising.

Sully was stunned. He could barely speak. He knew Molly by her voice and his mind began to race back to the time when he lived on the reservation. Yes, he and Molly did have sexual relations. But he wondered, could this be true? And why had she waited so long to tell him?

"Sully, you still there?" Molly was on her knees in the total darkness of the confessional. Maybe he slipped away from the other side of the dark curtain that hung between them. Was he that cowardly? Molly's rage began to rise. After years of her suffering. Holding this secret all by herself. Having a child and then giving her away. She was overwhelmed with anger and grief.

"I'm here," the priest said, "but I must remind you that it is a mortal sin to lie in confession."

"I'm not lying!" Molly screamed. "We had a child together!" Molly had expected Sully to be more understanding, to have compassion for her and their child.

"Shh," the priest pleaded as he began to take in the information. "Now, you say a good act of contrition and then the rosary for five days as your penance, but we will have to talk more about this after Mass."

Molly was furious. She got up from her knees, threw the confessional curtain aside and stormed out of the church. Edna Francis next in line wondered what on earth was going on. Molly was mumbling to herself, "How could that SOB have accused me of lying. After all that I have been through. Not even, 'I'm sorry.'" Molly thought she would make him sorry and she knew exactly how to do this.

Sully broke into a cold sweat. What was Molly Paul trying to accomplish? Was this an attempt at blackmail or was he really the father of her child? He had difficultly listening to the rest of the penitents who kneeled before him with their, "Bless me Fathers." He could barely listen to their sins when he knew he had such an enormous sin of his own. But deep down Sully felt he would find a way out of this. He had always been able to weasel his way out of tight spots. It was only Molly's word against his. What could she prove at this late date. Still, he knew just how powerful Molly Paul was. He had seen her in action. He watched what happened when she had put a curse on poor Bonnie Neptune. Out of the blue Bonnie got sick and no doctor ever found the reason or the cure. Would he become a victim of Molly's wrath?

In the meantime, Molly walked to the shore behind the church to gather her thoughts. She needed a plan and she needed one fast before Sully left. He would be gone in a day or two after the Mass and community meeting. An icy wind blew off the water. Molly tucked her frozen fingers into her pockets for warmth and there she found the note Jimmy had left on the kitchen table before he headed out to work. She had not had time to read it before now:

Dear Mol,

I know the fire is dying between us. I can't feel

you with me anymore. Ever since the Bingo Palace burned down something has changed. I also know you will call that weasel of a back stabbing holy roller priest. Why would you go and do that? He's no good Mol. Get rid of him before he dumps you again. I'm not gonna wait around anymore.

Your own sweet love, Jim.

"Oh shit!" Molly says to no one in particular. "I don't need this crap right now."

When the last penitent left the confessional, Fr. Sully rose to make his way to the sacristy of the old church and dress for Mass. When he passed the statue of St Anne, he decided to stop and pray. He knelt in front of the life-size statue and began his prayer, "Glorious St. Anne filled with compassion." But his mind began to wander, "Laden with the weight of my troubles." He could not concentrate on his prayer, but he continued in the rote way he had learned to pray, "I cast myself at your feet." I must have a plan, he thought. I'm sure she has one. She is probably composing a letter to the Bishop right now. But what proof would she have after all these years? Still, this could ruin me. It could even cause my expulsion from the priesthood. It is much stricter these days than in the past. He wondered what he would do without the priesthood. How could he survive? He'd never held another job in his whole life. Oh shit! Why did I return to this God forsaken place?

Sully leaned on the wooden altar rail, held his head in his hands and began to weep. He did not sob, but tears fell from his eyes and rolled down his cheeks. He thought he would contact the Bishop and tell him in his own words how he was tricked into coming back to Northpoint. But Sully realized suddenly that it was not the bishop's wrath that he feared, he was terrified of the wrath of Molly Paul.

The church filled quickly as word spread of the healing Mass throughout the reservation. Even a few people from Eastport heard that the "healing priest" had returned. Out of curiosity they, too, appeared for the Mass. The church was full and anticipation high. After Mass was said, the priest called people to the altar for healing. One at a time the elderly women approached the altar, some using canes and some needing help to walk. Everyone knew that when the holy spirit entered them, they would fall down, so several young men came forward to assist their fall. It was Susie Stanley, a devoted parishioner, who first stood before the priest. Fr. Sully raised his arms and with his right hand touched the forehead of the red-headed woman.

Susie immediately fell backward into the arms of the two young men who gently let her lie on the floor before the priest. Sully assumed that Susie would open her eyes and ask for assistance in getting to her feet. But this didn't happen. Susie lay there even as the next parishioner fell beside her. After a short time, Sully became concerned and knelt by Susie hoping that she would wake up. But she did not. He felt helpless. It was then that all hell broke loose at St. Anne's church. One of the young men who had come to assist was an EMT and he found Susie had no pulse. He immediately pulled out a cell phone and dialed 911. Susie lay there turning gray and cold. Within minutes, the EMT and another young man carried Susie out of the church and into an ambulance. They raced to the Calais hospital but an hour later Susie Stanley was pronounced dead.

10

MOLLY LEAVES NORTHPOINT

_____

After Fr. Francis Sullivan gave Susie Stanley a fatal heart attack with his healing touch, he was forced to seriously question his priestly abilities. He did not stay around to say her funeral mass; in fact the very evening of her demise, he was given an escort by tribal police off reservation land. He was also told in no uncertain terms that he must never return to the Northpoint reservation. In effect, Sully was banned from any contact with tribal members, including Molly Paul.

A cold northeast wind blew in off the waters of Passamaquoddy Bay as Sully drove his old, red Subaru down Rte 1 towards Machias and points south. Rain and sleet made driving treacherous to the point that when he did reach Machias, he considered pulling over and spending the night in a motel. But his desire to leave Washington County and Maine, and cross back into Massachusetts, pushed him to drive on. The small New England towns he passed along coastal Rte 1 were dark and uninviting. To save time, he crossed at Ellsworth and headed inland for the interstate highway. It is here that he met the darkest of darknesses. There are no lights along the highway and he prayed a moose or deer would not enter his path. Miles and miles of only darkness. His spirits lifted when the headlights of an oncoming vehicle brightened the night, only to pass him and leave him in the empty void of the dark night. He tried to pray but he could not. His mind began to wander back to the words of Molly Paul, "Father, did you know you are a father?" How could this be? He has a child of perhaps fifteen or sixteen, a son or a daughter, she didn't say. But where is this child?

Hours later at Kittery, he crossed the long suspension bridge that links the state of Maine with the state of New Hampshire. For a brief moment Sully had the urge to swerve to the edge of the bridge and plunge into the frigid waters of the Piscataqua River. But the little red Subaru held steady to Highway 95 and Sully breathed a sigh of relief knowing that Massachusetts was less than an hour's drive south. It took little more than forty-eight hours for Northpoint tribal police to notify the Bishop of the archdiocese of Boston and overseer of St Mary's Star of the Sea church of the death of Susie Stanley. But this news was inconsequential compared to Molly's disclosure of Fr. Francis Sullivan's inappropriate sexual activity. Within days of his return to St. Mary's parish, Sully was served notice that he was being sent to a retreat for wayward priests in northern New Mexico. He would remain there until "rehabilitated."

"New Mexico! Where in God's name is that?" Sully cried out. He was a New Englander born and bred. He had never ventured farther west than New York State where he had attended an ecumenical retreat many years ago. Everything he loved about living along the north Atlantic coast flashed before him. The small fishing villages of his parish: Beverly, Gloucester, Salem, and the quiet introverted people who inhabited them. He loved the seafood chowders and fried fish platters of scallops and clams and shrimp and baked cod and haddock. How could he leave everything that was familiar and dear to him? How could he survive so far from the sea?

Meanwhile, back at Northpoint Rez, Molly Paul retreated to a room in her small house perched along the shore and she would not leave that room for three days except to get a tiny bit of food, and water. Jimmy was away working in the lumberyard in Robbinston. She spoke to no one. Her time alone was spent plotting her next move. She wanted no distractions and relied on her dreams to guide her. She slept in daylight and at night took flight into the other realm. Nights she sang the old songs and prayed for guidance from the women who had come before her. Margaret Moore was her grandmother, a quiet strong woman who had helped Molly most of all to sort through her anger.

On the fourth day of her seclusion, Molly emerged from her room and immediately began packing her red cloth suitcase. Warm weather clothes, a pair of tennis shoes, her ceremonial dress, moosehide moccasins, and several long braids of sweetgrass filled the small bag. Then she wrote a note to Jimmy Shay:

Jim,

I'm leaving for awhile. You keep the home fires burning. The house is yours for now.

Love, Molly

Molly bundled herself in her long woolen coat, opened the door of her warm house and walked two miles on the highway that dissected her reservation to Perry where she caught a Trailways bus to Bangor. There was no shelter for the bus stop, just a dented metal sign. She flagged the bus down at 9:30 am. At Bangor, she changed buses and headed south to Logan international airport in Boston. In the time between buses, she called ahead and made a one way reservation on a flight from Boston to Dallas, Texas, and from Dallas on to Albuquerque, New Mexico. It would take her entire final paycheck from her job as bingo boss at Northpoint, but she didn't hesitate. From what she had seen and heard on her last visit to New Mexico, there were many tribal casinos and she was sure she could land a job at one of them. The important thing was for her to be with her sixteen-year-old daughter Kateri. Molly had given Kateri to a Pueblo woman sixteen years ago and now she was ready to meet her child.

It was a long trip to reach the airport in Boston and Molly knew she would need a good meal before she boarded her flight to the mountains and deserts of New Mexico. It had to be fish and fresh caught. She found a Boston Seafood Market restaurant and asked for a booth. She needed quiet to build her stamina for the long trip ahead. This was no time to lose her nerve. She considered a baked Maine lobster, but the price was way out of her range so she settled on a platter of baked filet of sole stuffed with crabmeat. She knew it would be a long while before she would be able to find fresh fish once she left New England. Molly ordered a glass of raspberry lemonade and waited for her fish to arrive. She was hungry. A strange man approached her booth.

"Excuse me, ma'am."

Molly looked up from her lemonade.

"Are you Indian?"

"Who's askin'?" Molly answered annoyed at the interruption.

"Just an ignorant white man who wants to know who you are and where you are going?"

"Well, before I tell you anything I want to know if you are FBI or a cop or a white man who hates Indians."

"None of the above," the red-headed man answered.

At this point Molly's fish platter arrived. The waitress eyed the man with suspicion as she placed the food before Molly.

"Everything all right here?" she asked.

Molly was in no mood for chitchat. She wanted to enjoy her fish and fly out of there. She didn't have time to be examined by some nosy intruder.

"I don't know this guy," she told the waitress

who gave the man a "bug off mister" look and he slowly walked away.

"Maybe somebody who had one drink too many," the waitress told Molly.

"Maybe," Molly muttered and began devouring her food.

"Anymore problems, you just let me know okay?" The waitress walked away.

The food was delicious. Molly realized that she had not eaten all day. When she was finished she paid her bill and left a $5 tip for the waitress. Her plane would board in a half hour and she needed to find the departing gate for her flight. Once on board the plane, night had fallen. The plane lifted and flew away from the foggy east coast. City lights became tiny specks in an endless void as the plane gained altitude.

Molly was ready now to face the Southwest and the challenges before her. She was excited about the prospect of seeing her daughter. She slept and returned to her dreams. She did not wake until the captain announced their approach to Dallas, Texas. At Dallas she had a two hour layover. She decided after some thought not to call ahead and give warning of her imminent arrival. Instead she would just take the shuttle bus at the airport to the casino in the pueblo where her daughter Kateri lives.

II

KATERI

———

Molly's daughter, Kateri Tekakwitha Paul, is sixteen-years-old but looks much older. She has dark brown, deep-set eyes and her red auburn hair reaches to her waist when she doesn't wear it braided. Her olive skin is much lighter than most of her classmates at Santa Fe Indian School where she attends 10th grade. She was a day student and rode the yellow bus each day the thirty miles from San Isidro Pueblo to Santa Fe.

She has lived at San Isidro for as long as she can remember. This year Kateri decided to dorm at school so on weeknights she sleeps there. It has not been an easy transition for her. Even with friends, she misses her large extended family: two older brothers and a younger sister and too many aunts, uncles and cousins to name. But she returns to the pueblo on weekends and holidays.

Kateri's mother, Juanita Velasquez adopted her when she was six-weeks-old. Juanita had no daughter and when Molly Paul asked her to take her infant girl, she happily agreed. It was a typical adoption in the Indian way with a giving ceremony but there was no paperwork, no exchange of money, just an agreement of trust between two women who had known each other since childhood.

Juanita works at the Casino Hollywood which is owned and operated by the pueblo of San Isidro. She works in what they call "the cage" as a cashier handling and sorting more money than she has ever seen in her life. It is a job, not the best but not the worst. It's close to home and when her car dies, Juanita can walk to work.

It puts food on the table with a little money leftover. Juanita's boyfriend Joe Candelaria is now absent from her life. She prefers to use the word *absent* when describing his unwillingness to help her raise their kids.

"We're better off without him," she told Molly. "Better to not have to put up with his drunkenness and bad temper."

Over the years Molly sent money when she was able to help Juanita care for Kateri. But often months would go by and Juanita would not hear from Molly. But Molly planned to change all that. She wanted to take responsibility for her daughter and to be a real mother. She wasn't sure how she would do this but she was determined. Kateri knew she was adopted. It was obvious to look at her. Juanita had told her that her real mother lived in the north. Nothing more and Kateri didn't ask.

Juanita was the only mother Kateri had known and the only one she loved and trusted. She was raised lovingly for the most part. She had no desire to leave the Pueblo village where she was raised, especially if it meant moving to the cold and unfamiliar north. She had heard stories from her cousins about northern Indians. How they looked like white people and didn't know their language. It didn't bother Kateri that she didn't look Pueblo. She had learned and understood the Keres language and was allowed to participate in Pueblo activities via Juanita's clan. She considered Juanita to be her mother in all ways.

Kateri did well at school. She made the honor roll and for the most part she stayed out of trouble. She did get suspended for two days earlier this year for handing out Ex-Lax to kids who teased her about being light skinned. She told them it was chocolate. Unfortunately for her, a teacher intervened and turned her in to the principal.

Kateri knew that she was named after Blessed Kateri Tekewitha, a Mohawk girl who was up for sainthood due to her courage and ability to endure great emotional and physical suffering when standing up for her beliefs. As a child, Kateri read the stories of Tekakwitha's life. How at age four her parents and baby brother died from smallpox and how she had survived but was terribly scarred and blinded by the disease.

Kateri often thought of Tekakwitha when she needed strength to make it through the trials of her own childhood. Juanita was there for her but she could not defend her when Pueblo children mocked her and called her "white girl."

Kateri had a way of deflecting negative energy away from herself. No one ever taught her to do this. It was as though she knew instinctively how to send it back to her attacker. Molly Paul also possessed this ability. Molly knew that protection was essential for survival, and she had developed an elaborate system of protection for herself that she wanted to share with her daughter.

At the airport in Albuquerque, Molly decided against renting a car. She needed to hold on to all the cash she had for whatever is next. Molly caught the shuttle bus from the Albuquerque Airport to the casino at San Isidro Pueblo. Waiting for the bus Molly was surprised by the heat of this city. Even in late September the temperatures were in the 90's, but the sun felt good to her. It burned heat into her bones. At home even in summer, the sun is never this warm. It is a short two-and-a-half mile ride to the San Isidro Pueblo and Molly watched as the Manzano and Sandia mountains are etched into a giant clear blue sky. The mountains look to her like moonscapes. She is used to the hills of New England with its abundance of trees, plants, and habitual green. Is this another planet with mountains without trees?

It's past supper-time as the shuttle bus pulls into the parking lot of Casino Hollywood, and she is tempted to go inside for the buffet, but the light is fading and Molly wants to see her daughter before the sun sets on this most important day. She puts the wheels down on her red cloth suitcase and begins the short walk from the casino into the village of San Isidro. Along the paved road she notice a complex of doublewide trailers that have sprouted up since her last visit. When she reaches a four-way stop just before the bridge, which spanned the Rio Grande, the road turns to dirt. That is the moment that her heart begins to race. Juanita's home is just on the other side of the bridge. She wondered again if she should have called first and worried that she should have warned them of her visit. But the smells of chili roasting turned her thoughts back to food. She really is hungry. Willows line the banks of the river on both sides. The red muddy water is nothing like the river waters of Maine which run clear most of the year. Here there is no seeing what the river holds.

Two teenage girls pass on the other side of the road undoubtedly headed to the store at the four-way stop. They wave to her and she waves back feeling more at ease. Everybody waves when they pass one another either on foot or in car or truck. It is the customary Indian wave just like at Northpoint. Sometimes while driving it is just a two finger wave barely lifting from the steering wheel but it is nonetheless an acknowledgment of another life. For just a moment Molly thinks about home. She left in such a rush without even a word of explanation. She is pretty sure that Jimmy is pissed off about now. She'll call in a couple days to let him know she is safe and where she is, if he even cares.

Juanita's home is a simple one-story adobe most likely built by her father or grandfather. The twelve-inch walls keep the heat out in summer and the heat in in winter. It stands in a small yard next to a horno, a dome-shaped adobe oven where Juanita bakes bread and pies for feasts. A shrinking pile of split cedar wood is piled against a cattle wire fence at the far side of the yard. A few tall sunflowers have sprouted up along the fence; they face the setting sun.

When Molly arrives at Juanita Velasquez's home, she is not prepared for the commotion that her visit will cause. Juanita is working at the casino and Kateri is home alone. Enchilada's warming in the oven, Kateri sits at the kitchen table reading. She hears a dog bark in the neighbor's yard and looks up from her book. She sees Molly and watches from her kitchen window as Molly Paul walks up the dirt driveway towards the adobe home.

"Who the hell is that? Not someone I know," Kateri mutters.

Molly takes a deep breath and approaches the door to Juanita's home. Kateri has moved from the kitchen window to the door way. She is curious about this stranger with the red suitcase raising dust. She does not wait for Molly's knock, but instead she opens the door and faces Molly. Kateri was away on a school retreat to the

Six Nations reservation in Canada when Molly visited Juanita last spring and they hadn't met.

Molly thinks it has been a long fifteen and a half years since she has seen her daughter. She never asked for photos over the years. She didn't want longing to set in and she wasn't ready until now to have her daughter in her life.

The two women look at each other for what to Molly is a too long and uncomfortable time, but Kateri is unmoved. It is rare here that a stranger approaches her door. She knows just about everyone in the small village of 500 Indians as well as people from other Pueblos. This is a stranger. Her skin is lighter than the people of San Isidro, and she does not look like a Pueblo Indian. Indian maybe, Kateri thinks, but not Pueblo. Finally, Molly speaks her daughter's name, "Kateri?" already knowing the answer.

"Yes, I'm Kateri. Who are you?"

Molly can feel the sweat beading on her upper lip and her heart begins to race. "I'm Molly Paul, a friend of Juanita's from the Northpoint reservation in Maine."

"Maine, that's far away," Kateri shoots back. "Juanita's at work but she should be back soon."

Kateri eyes Molly's red suitcase. "But come in. You can sit over there." Kateri points to a chair by the kitchen table. "Want something to eat? I was just going to have supper. I hate to eat alone."

Molly is relieved at the thought of food and does as directed. Kateri fills two plates with green chili chicken enchiladas and sets them on the table. "Want some Coke?" she asks her new guest.

"No, just water will be fine," Molly answers. Thinking how much Kateri does resemble her father. Kateri gets a glass of water for Molly then sits across from her at the small wooden table. They both eat in silence. Both wonder what is next. Then Kateri asks, "So what's it like to live in Maine?"

"Cold winters with deep snow and winds that will blow you over but summers are wonderful. Wild berries grow all around our reservation. We have acres and acres of wild blueberry fields and wild strawberries, raspberries, and blackberries, too. Everyone fishes and digs clams. Some of the guys have lobster boats. We have big feasts and dances in August. Our reservation is small. It is surrounded on three sides by water. In the fall, the men hunt moose and deer. The game is plentiful. Nobody starves there."

"How many people live there?"

"Less than 800. Everyone knows everyone."

"Any casinos?"

"Nope. We had a high stakes bingo hall but it burned. Now people gamble in the basement of St. Anne's church."

Kateri gets up to help herself to more food. A reservation without a casino, she thinks. That's weird. Mom should be home soon.

"Do you want more food?" Kateri asks Molly looking back from the oven.

"No thanks, I'm good." Molly pushes her chair back from the table. She knows it is rude to stare, but she can't take her eyes off her daughter. She has Sully's good looks, she tells herself. But she can see herself in her, too. She has my dark eyes and the way she moves is me. She is my daughter, but will she accept me? Molly wishes Juanita would come home. She needs to talk with her before breaking the news to Kateri.

"What time does Juanita usually get home?" Molly asks rising from the table.

"Is she expecting you?" Kateri asks.

"Well, not really. I guess I should have called her before coming."

Molly walks over to her suitcase, opens it, and takes a pair of intricately beaded moosehide moccasins from inside. "Here, these are for you," she tells Kateri. "Do you dance over here?"

Kateri is surprised by the gift. "Yes I dance. Social dances at powwows and sometimes here in the village."

"Well, if there are winter dances, these will keep your feet warm," Molly tells her.

"Thank you very much," Kateri takes the moccasins. She sits back at the table to try them on.

Kateri removes her lime green high top sneakers and puts her left foot into the beautiful beaded moccasin. Floral designs done with very small colored beads cover the top of the moccasins. They are lined with rabbit fur.

Unlike the Pueblo style moccasins, Molly is right; these will be very warm for winter dances. Kateri remembers hearing an elder in the village who told her, "We know where you come from by your moccasins."

"A perfect fit. How did you know my size?"

Just then Juanita comes through the door of her house. She sees Molly and takes a step back, then she looks at Kateri.

"Molly Paul! What a surprise! It looks like you and Kateri have met."

From the look on Juanita's face, Molly knows she should have called ahead. Maybe she should not have come here after all. Juanita is an aging Pueblo woman who wears her hair long and pulled back into a knot. Her long bangs, which she curls on plastic curlers each night, look out of place on her deeply lined face. Juanita has aged since Molly last visited her and her dark skin has lost its glow. She wonders if Juanita is sick. Her usual stocky build has diminished.

"Excuse me if I don't join you, I'm beat and I ate at the buffet. The casino is hopping. Don't know how much longer I can take this job. You look tired too, Molly. Kateri, you have school tomorrow. Let's just get some sleep."

"We can talk in the morning," Juanita says looking at Molly. "You can sleep in the spare room, the bed is made up. If you need anything just let me know." Juanita is annoyed, but she is too tired to deal with the situation.

The next morning after Kateri left for school, Juanita and Molly were left alone to talk.

"What are your intentions, Molly?" Juanita asks over coffee.

"Well, I'd like your advice Juanita, but I wanted to tell Kateri that I am her mother."

Juanita gave her an it's about time look then replied, "Why now?"

"It's time she knew. I want to know my daughter, maybe even take her home with me." Molly sees that she is on shaky ground and looks into her coffee cup.

Juanita feels her anger rising. She is trying to contain her wrath but she cannot. "Why, Molly Paul. Why would you want to upset things now. Kateri is doing well at school here. She loves living with the only family she has ever known. She has finally been accepted into my clan. Isn't it a bit selfish of you to come here now without a word of notice and drop a bomb on her like that? Just because YOU want to know YOUR daughter. It might be too little too late, Molly Paul." Juanita looks straight through Molly. "She is your daughter, but for the last sixteen years I've been the only mother she has ever known."

Molly is taken back by Juanita's ire. She is feeling her own guilt now. She wants out of the house. "I'm going out for a walk. We can talk later," Molly tells Juanita and she walks out the door.

Molly heads back over the bridge that crosses the Rio Grande, past the four way stop and into the parking lot of Casino Hollywood. As she walks, she tells herself it may have been a bad idea for her to have come for Kateri. Why would a teenager want to leave her friends and the only family she has ever known to go north with a woman who she doesn't know just because she says she is her mother? I've made a mistake, she tells herself as she walks towards the revolving doors of the casino. What now?

The rank smell of stale tobacco, the lack of

daylight and the loud noise of slot machines going wild overwhelms Molly. This is foreign territory. The closet thing to a casino she has ever known was the bingo hall at Northpoint. She knew everyone there but here she is a stranger. How would Kateri feel among strangers, she wonders.

Molly forces herself to sit at a machine. She is low on funds but she takes a ten dollar bill from her pocket and slips it into the slot machine. It is the Wild Red Rose game and she bets seventy five cents at a time. Two roses hit and she doubles her money. "What the hell," she says to herself and slides a twenty dollar bill into the machine. On the eleventh spin Molly hits big. Three roses, "O my god!" She can hardly believe it. She won five hundred dollars and without even knowing it. The machine lights up like a Christmas tree and bells and sirens go off. Next thing she knows a slot attendant is standing next to her. "Not bad for ten bucks," she tells the guy. "Where do I cash this out?"

"Right over here, Ma'am," he points to a cashier window at the back of the casino. Molly leaves Casino Hollywood. She has made her decision to return home to Northpoint. "I don't belong here," she mutters.

At Juanita's no one is home but the door is unlocked. Molly uses the phone to make a plane reservation back to Boston. Then she writes Juanita a note:

Sorry,

My mistake.

I'm going home.

– Molly

Molly leaves Juanita's and crosses the Rio Grande with her red suitcase in tow. "Muddy ol' river," she mumbles and tells the river. "I like my waters clear." Molly waits at the casino for the shuttle to take her to the airport. She has plenty of time to think about her visit. If only Sully had not been such a coward. They could have visited Kateri together. He would have loved her. But that is all water over the dam now. Molly regretfully decides to move on. She boards a plane to Boston then catches the Greyhound bus to Maine. In sixteen hours she is back at Northpoint.

Autumn has painted brilliant red, yellows, and oranges into maples, oaks, and birches.

Frost helped itself to everything still growing in backyards. The people eat fish chowders and dream of deer and moose stews. Piles of firewood once again appear in dooryards. The same broken down Indian cars and pickups stand watch. Northpoint and its people prepare themselves for hurricanes and northeast storms.

But even with winter approaching, Molly Paul is happy to be home. She just walks into her house as though she had been down to Old Town for a couple days. Jimmy Shay nearly drops his Budweiser when he sees Molly in the doorway.

"Well look what the cat dragged in," Jimmy smiles ear to ear.

"I'm beat," Molly tells him. "I'm going to bed now."

"OK Mol. Glad you're home. We can talk later."

12

AIRLINE

———

It was the year when pilot whales beached themselves in great numbers. Pod after pod came ashore, got trapped and died. The Indians called them "black fish." They said the whales were telling us to pay attention to the water. Pollution had made water unlivable and the whales were considering coming back to live on the land as they had done many, many years ago.

That same year, Viola Dana got her bloods

again at age 60 after ten years of menopause. She got checked out at the clinic, even went to the hospital in Calais for an ultrasound. They found nothing wrong with her. The doctors told her she was a "miracle woman" and could once again conceive.

"No way," she told him. "I've had all the kids I need in one lifetime." That was seven.

Then the snowy owls came to live at Northpoint in unusually high numbers. In the past, a rare pair or a single owl might come down from Canada to visit each year but now four pairs had returned that winter to mate on the Northpoint rez. Francis Sockebesin, tribal wildlife officer, said the earth's electromagnetic field had been disrupted by too much air and space travel which caused the birds to not remember where they were. But in truth, nothing was the same. We never knew from one day to the next what might happen.

At the Wabanaki Grill, the talk was all about who would win the world series: Red Sox or Yankees. Most people are Red Sox fans but Eddie Francis insists on defending the Yanks. The stakes were never higher. He waged his scalloping nets against Brian Paul's dingy. No one had any money of course and scalloping season was called off this year due to over-fishing of the beds, so it didn't really matter who won after all. At least for now. Eddie's special of the day: grilled mooseburger with fries and a Coke for $3.99. All the guys are enjoying their burgers when in strolls Molly Paul and Viola Dana.

"Well look what the cat dragged in," Brian mutters under his breath, "if it ain't Molly Paul."

All heads turn towards the door to check out the two women. Molly wears a jean jacket and a black hoodie over one of her boyfriend, Jimmy Shay's, flannel shirts. Her blue jeans are spotless and on her feet she wears rubber mud boots. Viola also wears jeans and a black sweatshirt with the Northpoint Tribe seal printed on the front. On the back the words "Indian and Proud." She is much taller than Molly but walks a few paces behind her. She allows Molly to make the grand entrance.

"Where you been, Mol?" Eddie faces Molly. "Haven't seen you in a month or two."

"Oh, I've been traveling. Have to get away

from this place every now and then in order to appreciate home."

"Bet they didn't have mooseburgers where you went. Can I get you today's special?"

"Sure, make mine well done. How do you want yours Vi?"

"Same," Vi answered, "but no Coke for me, I want coffee, black."

"Be right up." Eddie turns to go back behind the grill.

Molly knows there will be questions about her travels but she prefers to keep the details to herself. However, the moccasin telegraph has been ticking away at Northpoint where most people are related in one way or another and secrets are hard to keep. Molly and Viola grew up together at Northpoint. Over the years their friendship had been tried and tested many times, especially during those years when Father Francis Sullivan was around. But overall, Molly feels she can trust Vi to keep her mouth shut about her intimacies, especially if she stresses CONFIDENTIALITY. No one knew Molly had just visited her grown daughter. She kept it silent and she preferred to keep it that way. She had just told Vi she had visited friends in New Mexico where the weather was warmer. Nothing more.

The two women take seats at the counter and wait for their burgers. "Hey gals, have you heard what happened to Bob Cat last night?" Eddie asks while he flips their burgers.

Molly and Vi look at eat other. "No, what happened to Bob. He drinks so bad, did someone take advantage of him in his drunken state?" Molly asks.

"Yup, a bunch of kids," Eddie answers.

"Well, what did they do to him this time?" Vi asks.

"Nearly burned Bob alive, that's what."

"Who, where, and how?" Molly fires back.

"Well, I heard Uggie Tomah and Jimmy Cleaves got a hold of a couple of gallons of kerosene and set his shack on fire with him passed out inside."

"Oh my God, did they kill him?"

"No, but almost. He's in Calais Hospital with third degree burns."

"How'd you find out, Ed?" Molly asks.

"Over the police radio. I hear everything on that thing."

"Jeez, what was the motive?" Vi questions, unable to believe her ears.

"Well, the boys said they did it because Bob was stealing their stash."

"Stash, stash of what?"

"Booze, of course. Those kids had packed away everything from Red Rose Wine and Smirnoff's vodka to mouthwash and hand sanitizer in that old bait shack near Francis Point."

"Hand sanitizer!" Vi yells. "What the hell do they do with that?"

"Drink it," Eddie laughed. "Didn't you hear about Uggie getting kicked out of rehab last month 'cause he and some other bird brain from Indian Island made hooch out of hand sanitizer and oranges?"

"Oh my God!" Molly sputters. "What is this world coming to?"

"No good," Eddie answers, handing over their burgers and fries.

"Hey Mol," Vi asks. "How about we drive down to Indian Island for Bingo tomorrow.

Those Penobscots have high stakes and if we win we'll be all set for winter?"

"Ya, Jimmy lost his job at the lumberyard and is talking about moving back to the Island. We could stay over with his sister. It's too far to drive back the same night. Bingo doesn't get out till the wee hours. It's a three hour drive back here. I heard Stella Neptune won big last weekend and got so excited she got right up and danced on the table."

"And Stella's no lightweight. Did the table hold her?" Molly laughs all the while eyeing her mooseburger.

"OK. Let's go! Plan to leave tomorrow around noon. I'll call Jimmy's sister. I'm sure it will be OK to stay over in her trailer. But we might have to sleep on the couch," Molly tells Vi.

The next day Vi drives over to Molly's place at noon as planned. It is snowing, a dry snow that barely sticks to the ground. But the temperatures have dropped to below freezing even at midday. Vi knows a storm is blowing up the coast and the prediction is for a foot or more of snow before nightfall. Snow in October is not unusual in down-east Maine. In fact, one of the worst blizzards of all time blew in on Columbus Day. But this doesn't deter her. She has good rubber on the tires of her truck and a little snow has never stopped her from doing what she wanted to do. It'll be good to have some time alone with Molly, Vi thinks, it's been a long time since they have had a heart-to-heart talk. Molly is waiting for her on the porch of her little house. Jimmy Shay's pickup is parked in the driveway. It is packed with boxes and a few pieces of furniture.

"Jim movin' on?" Vi asks Molly when she slides into the passenger seat of the truck, pointing with her lips at his pickup.

"Yup. After he lost his job at the lumberyard, he decided to move back to his own place at Indian Island. It's closer to Bangor where he's likely to find work, maybe at Home Depot he told me."

"Well, you'll miss him Mol," Vi pried.

Molly did not respond.

"You're looking tired Mol."

"Didn't sleep good last night," Molly answers.

"Are you sure you still want to make the trip?"

"For sure," Molly assures her.

They head south off reservation land to the highway. "Should we take the coastal route or head down the airline, route 9?" Vi asks Molly.

"Airline is quicker and with this storm coming we'd better get there sooner rather than later," Molly warns.

"Okay. Rte 9 Airline, here we come."

The four lane highway is called the Airline because truckers use it to haul lumber and other goods from Bangor to the Canadian border at Calais. It is a path that was cut through interior Washington County Maine and allows travelers to avoid the winding two lane coastal Rte 1 and the many towns situated along the coast. Few towns have been built along the Airline and it is lined on both sides by thick forests of pine and balsam fir. But with mile after mile of uninhabited land that stretches before them, both women know that even in good weather, the Airline can be a dangerous road to travel.

It has started to snow heavy now and Vi has the windshield wiper turned to high and the heater on full blast to keep the windshield clear. Snow blows sideways across the highway and Vi has a tight grip on the steering wheel to keep the truck on the road.

"Did you hear the weather forecast?" Vi asks Molly.

"Nope, but you know those guys are never right anymore. Weather patterns are so crazy no one can forecast it."

Molly reaches to turn on the truck radio, hoping they can get a report on the road conditions ahead.

She fears they are approaching a "whiteout." Inside the cab of the pickup Molly smells the sweet scent of sweetgrass. She assumes that Vi has a braid in the glove box.

The radio is full of static. "Must be the storm, even AM doesn't come in," Molly says annoyed. She opens the glove box and takes the sweetgrass braid out and places it on the dash of the truck.

"Vi, I've got something to tell you, but you have to swear that it won't leave the cab of this pickup."

"Sure, Mol, what's up?" Vi responds without lessening her grip on the steering wheel.

"I've got a grown daughter. Her name is

Kateri and she lives in New Mexico with some Indians there. Remember Fr. Francis Sullivan? Sully. He's her father but he has never seen her. That's where I was last month, in New Mexico."

"Oh my god Mol! A daughter. I'd never have guessed. I know there was some talk about you and Fr. Sully back then, but a baby girl?"

Swirling snow continues to make it more difficult for Vi to see ahead of her. She has turned the headlights to low beam in an attempt to foresee what the road has in store. But it is no use, they are in a complete whiteout.

"Think we should pull over?" Molly asks.

"That would be crazy, we might never get going again." Vi is worried now. "What we need is a snow plow ahead of us. But fat chance of that. You know how they just let the truckers plow the Airline."

There are no trucks on the road from what the two women can see. In fact, they hadn't seen another vehicle in what seemed like hours.

"I'll try to call ahead to Jimmy's sister and ask what the weather is like on the island," Molly tells Vi. She pulls a cell phone out of her jacket pocket. When she opens the phone, she realizes that they are in a dead zone. The screen reads *No Network Available.* "Forget that," she tells Vi. "No reception."

Vi has slowed the truck down to 30 mph or less. Any faster and she'd have trouble staying on the snow packed and icy highway. She had wanted to have a peaceful and relaxing ride to Indian Island. Time to talk with Molly about her trip to New Mexico and to ask her how she felt about Jimmy leaving. They'd been shacked up for more than ten years but now all of her attention needed to be on driving. Molly appeared to be restless sitting next to her, like she anticipated trouble.

It happened in an instant. Out of nowhere a huge mass of fur, bones, and antlers collided with the truck. There was no time to turn away, no time to stop. Vi's truck hit the moose in the legs. A huge bull moose whose knees reach the hood of the truck. Over he goes onto the windshield and top of the cab. More than 1,000 pounds of moose stops the two women in their tracks. Broken glass from the windshield everywhere.

The moose slides off the truck and lays

wounded on the snow-packed road. He lifts his massive head and raises himself up on his front legs before he lays back down to die. The truck has stalled out. Vi is pinned by the steering wheel and is unable to move her lower body. She notices the sweetgrass braid which has fallen into her lap. It is green and fresh and she can faintly smell the sweet aroma of the grass. She and her oldest daughter had packed a picnic on a hot day in August and spent the day at Lubec gathering the grass. Vi focused on her breathing and realized that she could move her arms. If only the steering wheel didn't have her pinned she could open the door of the truck. Then she looks over at Molly who is quiet in the passenger seat beside her, her head slumped to the side as if she had fallen asleep.

"Are you dead, Mol? We ran into a moose," Vi tells her. "I couldn't see it. There was no time to stop or to turn." Vi tells her quietly as if it was her fault that they hit the moose.

Molly does not respond. Vi notices a cut on Molly's forehead. Blood is trickling across her eye brow and down her cheek like a tear.

There is a bottomless silence that surrounds

the two women, the dying moose, the broken truck. The wind is silent, but snow continues to fall. It is Jimmy Shay who discovers the two women. He has his trucked packed and is moving to Indian Island and takes the same route as Molly and Vi. He left just a half-hour after the women were on their way.

Snow started early that year and it continued into springtime. The October blizzard covered the earth and storm after storm barreled up the coast.

In June, the earth finally began to green. Wild strawberries appeared in record numbers in the fields around Northpoint. They were so plentiful that year that Eddie Francis had strawberry shortcake on the menu at the Wabanaki cafe. First time ever.

13

EPILOGUE

"After the moose and Vi's truck collided, I first thought moose meat for the freezer! But then I realized I wasn't moving and then I wasn't breathing and my heart had stopped. Shit! I thought I must have had a heart attack. I don't feel any pain but there is all this white light around. I am floating through it, there is no end and I have no destination. I know I am traveling because my long braid has come undone and my hair is flying behind me. So that's that. Cancer didn't get me. A traveling moose stopped me in my tracks. Now I won't have to face Jimmy Shay with the truth about Kateri being my daughter and well, I won't have to face Kateri about that slime bag Fr. Francis Sullivan being her dad. I won't have to face Bonnie Neptune knowing it was me who put the whammy on her. I tried to take it back but things don't work like that. I should have known better. It almost killed her. Old Greg saw it all even though they say he is blind. He told me to back off but I didn't know how. Sometimes death solves everything. Over and out." —Molly Paul

14

WINTER FREEZING RAIN

I don't know how Viola Dana managed to track me down. Something about Jimmy Shay finding Juanita's phone number in my mother's things. Anyhow, I got the call the day after she passed away and the next day I was on a plane to the cold north woods and waters of Northpoint. We had just finished roasting corn in the adobe ovens at San Isidro. The whole village participated: women, children, and men all shucking the cobs of the roasted corn, tending the fires, making sure everything went just right. The whole village smelled of roasted corn. It was my favorite time of year. But I am my mother's only kin and I needed to go there. Juanita said it wouldn't be right not to go.

Winter freezing rain. Fourth night of the wake, we have been sitting with you day and night. My ice cold mother with your jet black hair pulled back in a long braid, an eagle feather in your right hand, sweetgrass braid in the other. We are praying and singing to help you on your journey to the other side. Tonight the whole village comes together in the basement of St. Anne's Catholic church where Bingo is held on Sunday nights and on Wednesday nights, Sr. Monica, a very old nun, teaches catechism classes to the young.

The new priest, Fr. Jack O'Connor, known by everyone here as the "one who eats at every home he visits" sits at a long table by the wood stove where Jimmy Shay, Viola Dana, and her three young children and I also sit. It is the "last supper" for you. We eat fry bread and cornbread with fresh fish soup, baked beans, macaroni and cheese, hulled corn soup and moosemeat stew. For dessert, molasses cake and blueberry pies. The priest prays over the food and when we have finished eating, Lilly Paul, the oldest woman of the tribe, blesses us all. Her long white braid reaching to her waist, she paints our faces with the signs that say we have mourned and now our tears must stop. It is near midnight and tomorrow the men will carry your casket up the hill from the church to the cemetery. Most of us will follow on foot, the elderly and sick will be driven in pickup trucks. Then the earth will receive you. But tonight the scent of wood smoke, cedar, sage and sweet grass carries me off to sleep. You will come to me in dreams. And Vi tells me at dawn the loon will cry on the river.

After the burial, a thick fog moved in as if to hide what had occurred at Northpoint. People moved around slowly for fear they would collide with someone or something unseen. The waters of the bay disappeared altogether and unless you stood right at the shoreline, it was impossible to see where the land ended and water began. Surrounded on three sides by water the reservation seemed isolated from the mainland.

Even the bridge to Eastport was impassable. People feared they would drive off the sides, unable to see their way. The white line in the middle of the road had disappeared. But in the dense fog, sound travelled very well. The foghorn at the lighthouse at Quoddy head sounded as though it was close, very close, even though it was many miles away.

I stand on the porch of my mother's three-room house. Raised in the desert southwest, I've never known the cold that settles into my bones here. I shiver and my teeth chatter wearing only a jean jacket and a hoodie I brought with me. It is burgundy and has the Santa Fe Indian School emblem and a feather painted on the sleeve. I have never heard the sound of a foghorn. It is a low wailing that travels over the water to warn sailors that the passage is dangerous and to stay away.

I was born here but I don't know a soul here. I didn't even know my mother until last month when she came to find me in New Mexico. But at her funeral I look around and see myself in many of the faces of the people of Northpoint. Many of us have light eyes, even reddish hair and fair skin, unlike the brown dark eyed people of the pueblo where I was raised. It is a feeling I have never known, to share genes, blood and bones. To share identity yet to feel like an outsider.

Jimmy Shay told me that everything in my mother's house is mine. Her clothes, her regalia, even the little house with all its contents is mine. I turn from the cold northeast wind and enter my home. Jim built a fire in the wood stove before leaving this morning to return to his village, Indian Island. I stand by the fire warming myself and wonder if I'd fit into any of my mother's warm clothes. If I'd want to. I am a desert dweller. My eyes always turn to the sky. Here, people have a horizontal gaze. Those who live by the sea look ahead, not over head. They know that life continues with the turning of the tides and that one day water will cover all that they have known. The old people speak of this often in a land where the sun often is not seen for days, even weeks.

Over at the WAB, the tribal café, Viola, Dana, and Eddie Francis ponder my fate. "She's so young, she can't live alone," Vi tells Eddie.

"Who will watch over her and tend to her needs? Make sure she doesn't get into trouble, and we all know how much trouble there is to get into at Northpoint." Vi had pleaded with Jimmy Shay before he left. "Won't you consider staying until she gets settled?" But the thought of looking after a teenage girl who he knew not at all, did not appeal to Jim. He was determined to go back to live at Indian Island, his home.

"Who knows how long she'll stay with us?" Eddie asked Vi. "After all, she has a family and friends down there in the hot desert. She might leave."

"She won't," Vi shot back. "She is one of us, she'll stay."

I fit perfectly into my dead mother's clothes. I like her black and red wool hunting jacket, and with her hoodie underneath I was plenty warm. I wore Molly's black rubber gum boots with two pairs of socks to keep my feet warm. Vi stayed overnight with me for a week after Jimmy left to show me around Molly's house and to introduce me to some people at Northpoint. But Vi needed to tend to her own family and moved back to her home up the hill. I was fine with staying alone. Vi made sure I would come to her house for dinner every evening and told me I could even stay there if I wanted. It was after Vi went back to her home and I was alone in the house when the dreams began. At first I didn't pay attention to them. I tried not to remember what I had dreamed. I had no memory of my infancy when I lived in this house with my mother. No memory of the tides coming and going, of the salt air, of the water that was all around me. I felt like a stranger at Northpoint even if I was born here.

On the second night in the house alone, Molly appeared to me. It started in dreams. I dreamed Molly had taken me into a deep marshland near the reservation to gather sweetgrass. The marsh was wet and filled with bloodsucking mosquitos that were merciless in their attack on me. Molly didn't seem to notice them at all. Molly wanted to show me how to pull sweetgrass by its purple roots and tie it in large bundles which she would store in her house after hanging them to dry. Molly pleaded with me for help but I resisted and tried to run away from my mother. I was afraid of the tides and was very uncomfortable at the water's edge. I refused, Molly insisted. Molly took hold of me and dragged me into the marsh.

"No. I won't go!" I yelled as I sat up in my bed. I reached for a cigarette to calm myself. Viola had refused to talk about my father when I asked her straight out, "Who is my father? Where does he live? Why hadn't he attended Molly's funeral?" Viola just shrugged and said, "I don't know any of that." But a few days later, Vi took me over to meet old, blind Greg. She hoped he'd have answers for my questions and help me to feel more comfortable at Northpoint.

Greg is sitting at his kitchen table drinking Lipton tea and "watching" the sea from the window which overlooks the bay. His kitchen is warm from the wood fire that burns in his kitchen stove. His walls are bare except for one old photograph that hangs near the window. It is of Greg as a young man standing in a large birch bark canoe leaning against a wooden paddle.

Although Greg is legally blind, he insists that he can read the weather by watching the sea and the sky. Most of the fishermen at Northpoint consult with him before going out to sea on long trips into the treacherous waters of the North Atlantic and the Grand Banks of Newfoundland. Greg has proven never to be wrong with his forecasts. He has even saved some lives. He never charges for his services, just asks to be paid in fish.

Northpoint reservation is on a peninsula that protrudes into Passamaquoddy Bay. I knew I would refuse to ever step onto a boat. I was reluctant to even walk too close to the shoreline for fear I might be swept away. I don't know how to swim. Vi pulled a chair up to Greg's small kitchen table and beckoned for me to sit.

"Want tea?" Greg asked.

"Not me," Vi answered. "I have to run over to the Super Saver in a minute. You need anything Greg?" Without waiting for him to answer she asked, "Kateri, how about you?"

Greg told Vi he was all set, and I mostly ate at Vi's so I said I couldn't think of anything I needed. With that Vi walked out the door and left Greg and I sitting and watching the sea.

"You ever been to sea?" Greg asks me.

"No, never. I can't swim. I never even saw the ocean until I came here. It scares me."

Greg looks puzzled then he tells me stories of whales and sea monsters that used to come into the Passamaquoddy Bay. "No one remembers the songs to call them anymore. So they don't come now," he tells me as my eyes grow big listening to Greg. "This will all be water soon."

I light a cigarette and blow the smoke away from Greg. "A flood?" I ask.

"Yep, all water. The tides are getting higher and higher. Someday the water will cover Northpoint."

"Holy!" I mutter. "How do you know this?"

"I know. We've known this forever. Everybody knows. It's just a matter of time. Look at the first and second islands and how much they have sunk in just a few years. It's happening faster now," Greg points to the two islands in the bay.

I am very uncomfortable with the idea of a sunken Northpoint. I stand and look directly at Greg. "Well, I better go home now, check my fire, it's getting colder," as I pull my jacket on and zip it. I thank Greg and walk out the door. I hope his stories don't give me bad dreams.

It is dusk and I want to be home before dark. As I walk in the cold air, I realize that there is smoke in the air. I assume it is coming from the chimneys of most of the houses along my path. Nights are cold now and I worry that the fire in my wood stove has gone out in my absence. But as I pass the elderly center and St. Anne's Church, the smoke grows thicker.

"This is someone's house," I mutter as I take a red bandana from my jacket pocket and tie it over my nose and mouth. Sirens screech and I realize there is a house fire on the rez. The fire department at Northpoint is all volunteer and men are running into the street. Pickup trucks are racing by me to get to the fire. "Where's the fire?" I yell, but no one answers so I run with them. Soon I realize that I am running towards my own home, the house that Molly left me. When we round the corner, I see my home totally engulfed in flames.

The front porch has collapsed and the roof is ablaze. Asphalt shingles add fuel to the fire. It is an inferno, the heat so intense I have to step back. Firefighters are working hard to put out the fire, but it is too late. In a short time the house burns flat. Only the granite stones of the foundation remain. They are blackened with soot.

By now, most of the village has come to help and to watch. I see Viola Dana standing alone and I approach her. "What happened?" I ask Vi.

"Not sure, but you probably had a chimney fire and no one was home to call for help."

"Vi, do you smell that?"

"Yup," Vi looks at me. "Molly had a huge stash of sweetgrass bundles stored in the upstairs bedroom. Every year she would add to it. It was a ritual for her. It's all gone now."

About The Author

Barbara Robidoux

Barbara Robidoux is the author of two books of poetry *Waiting for Rain* (2007) and *Migrant*

Moon (2012). Her fiction has appeared in the *Denver Quarterly*, *The Yellow Medicine Review*, the *Santa Fe Literary Review*, and numerous anthologies. *SWEETGRASS BURNING* is her first collection of short stories.

She holds a BA from the University of New Hampshire, an MA from Vermont College and is currently a candidate for an MFA in creative writing from the Institute of American Indian Arts. She lives in Santa Fe, New Mexico where she is currently at work on a novel. She is of Eastern Cherokee (Tsalagi), Italian and Scottish heritage.

Acknowledgements

The stories *The Edge* and *Ghosts of Chibesquiog* have previously appeared in the Yellow Medicine Review. Fall 2013 and Fall 2014 respectively.

Cast of Characters

Main characters:

DOUS—A young Passamaquoddy woman narrator for first part of book. She is without parents, has no siblings or children. Best friend of Bonnie and is her birthing partner.

PEG—An ELDERLY Passamaquoddy woman who suffers from cancer, lives alone at Elderly

Center and is befriended by Dous — Only appears in first story The Edge.

GREG—a very old Passamaquoddy man who was once a fisherman. He has "the sight" but is legally blind. Lives mostly in his visions. Alone in his small home no family.

BONNIE NEPTUNE—friend of Dous, mother of Ricky, is very sick with mysterious illness. Daughter of Edna.

RICKY NEPTUNE—son of Bonnie. Born with a caul. A fisherman and drug dealer. Roams away from the rez then returns.

MOLLY PAUL—a woman pushing age 60, Bingo boss, who uses her psychic powers for evil at times. Mother of Kateri Paul.

Father FRANCIS SULLIVAN—A Charismatic (as in born again) Catholic priest who was priest at St Anne's on rez but is banned after someone dies when he tries to heal her. Father of Kateri Paul.

KATERI PAUL—sixteen year old daughter of Molly Paul who was given away as an infant.

JIMMY SHAY—A Penobscot Indian who is a long time boyfriend of Molly Paul and lives at Northpoint.

VIOLA DANA—long time friend of Molly Paul.

SNOOP SISTERS— three elderly sisters who roam the rez: Edna, Helen, Grace Francis.

Minor Characters:

JUANITA VELASQUEZ— Kateri's adoptive mother.

EDDIE FRANCIS—Proprietor of the Wabanaki Grill and cook.

SIMON—Ricky Neptune's friend.

Drug Man Unnamed—man in restaurant to whom Ricky sells drugs.

About Blue Hand Books

For more great books by our Native authors,
visit Blue Hand Books at
www.bluehandbooks.org and please tell your
friends.

You can help our writers if you leave an honest review on Amazon.com.

Made in the USA
San Bernardino, CA
26 February 2016